"We're bad

"Are we?" Alex ask[...] her face.

"You go off and leave me, make your life elsewhere, yet you're in everything I do. It's destroying my life."

"Scott, don't say that! I'll go away. Is that what you want?"

He laughed discordantly. "If it would work." He glanced down at Alex's flushed face and saw her distress. "Come here to me." He lifted his arm so she could fit herself into his side. So long since he had lain with her. An eternity. Yesterday. "The minute you're able you'll do what you did before. You'll go off. Back to your career. Your life with me was just make-believe."

"No!"

"What if I made you pregnant?" he said harshly. "What if I played the same rotten game women play on men? I want a child. Our child. I want a part of you. Part of me. That way I'll always get to keep you."

Margaret Way takes great pleasure in her work and works hard at her pleasure. She enjoys tearing off to the beach with her family on weekends, loves haunting galleries and auctions and is completely given over to French champagne "for every possible joyous occasion." Her home, perched high on a hill overlooking Brisbane, Australia, is her haven. She started writing when her son was a baby, and now she finds there is no better way to spend her time.

Books by Margaret Way

Don't miss any of our special offers. Write to us at the following address for information on our newest releases.

Harlequin Reader Service
U.S.: 3010 Walden Ave., P.O. Box 1325, Buffalo, NY 14269
Canadian: P.O. Box 609, Fort Erie, Ont. L2A 5X3

Holding on to Alex
Margaret Way

Harlequin Books

TORONTO • NEW YORK • LONDON
AMSTERDAM • PARIS • SYDNEY • HAMBURG
STOCKHOLM • ATHENS • TOKYO • MILAN
MADRID • WARSAW • BUDAPEST • AUCKLAND

ISBN 0-373-03476-8

HOLDING ON TO ALEX

First North American Publication 1997.

Copyright © 1997 by Margaret Way Pty. Ltd.

This edition published by arrangement with Harlequin Books S.A.

® and TM are trademarks of the publisher. Trademarks indicated with
® are registered in the United States Patent and Trademark Office, the
Canadian Trade Marks Office and in other countries.

Printed in U.S.A.

CHAPTER ONE

LONG shadows were stalking the wild bush country before McLaren rode out, signalling to Abe his senior stockman to hurry up. Abe looked a mess, his deeply seamed face tired and disgruntled. All day long they had been tracking The Ghost, the brumby stallion that had been stealing the best of the station mares. In the harsh glare of noon they had sighted him running hard, his harem bunched up tightly behind him, a few yearlings bringing up the rear. A dozen horses in all and a stirring sight as they galloped recklessly down a steep, stony hill face and into the sanctuary of the vine-shrouded lignum. He could smell the sweat off their hides as his own blood began racing. He and Abe had given chase, branches racking their faces, raising blood as they rode into the stallion's home territory. Personal safety was a small thing compared to capturing the stallion. Both of them expert horsemen with some of the brumby's own recklessness, they had started to close, no mean feat in the scrub. Loving horses as he did, McLaren felt a stab of pity at the thought of depriving the big chalky grey of its freedom but The Ghost was no ordinary brumby. He was a fine-looking animal with good station blood in him. The thing was he had to be stopped. Abe could break him in and if Abe couldn't do it he'd have a go himself. Both of them knew how to get into the mind of horses. He had learned almost everything he knew from Abe Eagle Owl, yet as Abe freely admitted now, McLaren was master.

Even so, they lost them. The stallion won out. He was

enormously cunning. Three times he had beaten them although on the second chase they had picked up two station mares, both of them heavily pregnant. As always with wildlife, the stallion sensed danger even before it became apparent. What's more, the stallion knew this stretch of country even better than they did.

"Cunnin' bastard," Abe swore as he rode alongside, his ebony skin covered with sweat, streaks of blood and grit. A wind had got up, sending dust devils right at them. "I did my best, Boss."

"Hell, it's not your fault, Abe," McLaren sighed heavily, pulling off his akubra and raking an impatient hand through hair as black and shiny as a magpie's wing. "We'll get him in the end." He veered off right to avoid a pair of little grey wallabies, faces as sweet and innocent as babies. "Meanwhile, we'll set about building a trap closer in to the swamp. Behind that wall of tea trees." He gestured with an inclination of his head. "And make it *strong*."

"Plenty strong," Abe growled, weary to the point where he felt he could fall out of the saddle. "The Ghost's a wild one. I'm thinkin' a rogue."

McLaren shook his head. "There's good blood in him, Abe. He'll behave once he knows who's boss." He suddenly realised with a pang he had pushed Abe too hard. Although always willing, Abe wasn't as young as he used to be.

The sunset revived them, breathtaking in its beauty. It swept across the gleaming cobalt sky leaving great billowing trails of rose, violet and gold before the Sun Woman turned the world to molten fire and the distant sand hills glowed like hot furnaces. Abe with a rich Dream life within him and the music of the most ancient of cultures began a soft, deep chant that McLaren found wonderfully tranquillising; rising and falling it was an incantation that echoed through the mists of time. He had enjoyed Abe's company since he was a small boy and his father had told him Abe Eagle Owl was a lawgiver and a man of great power and magic. According to the desert aborigines, Abe could weave mighty spells. McLaren knew for a fact Abe could sing in the rain. His father had trusted and respected the tribal elder, setting him to watch over his only son and heir.

"To guard you, Scotty, from possible harm."

Abe, the powerful medicine man, hadn't been able to guard his father. John McLaren had ridden out one morning, vital, handsome, a man in his prime, respected by the whole Outback, worshipped by his son, only to be carried back to the homestead on a makeshift stretcher, his neck at a terrible angle, broken in a freak fall. *This* the end to a man who had lived all his life in the saddle, a man acknowledged to be a splendid horseman. It was really too much.

It had broken his mother's heart. For maybe two years. Maximum. After that, she had found herself another rich husband and gone away. As a dutiful son, he had continued to visit her in the city to pay his respects, but he had never forgiven her for her defection, nor for so easily forgetting his father.

He'd been fourteen when his father was killed. Fourteen was a vulnerable sometimes dangerous age for a boy, even if he had looked and acted like a young man. That's what the mantle of responsibility and high parental expectations did to one. But he had still needed his mother; the mother who felt she couldn't possibly live out the rest of her life in isolation no matter how splendid. She had to go back to the city, to her own people, to her own kind of life.

That was when Wyn had come back to Main Royal. Edwina McLaren, his father's elder sister, unmarried, a woman of great character with a successful career writing and illustrating stories with an Outback theme for older children. Wyn had been enormously popular for twenty-five years and more. Loving, patient, ever supportive Wyn. The mother he had never really had.

As he and Abe rode companionably side by side, great flights of birds winged over them, their colours brilliant like flowers, making for the lagoons and billabongs. Once a shining formation of budgerigars circled them, dipping and swooping overhead like an undulating wave of emerald silk shot with gold.

Magic!

But even as he looked up, another image invaded his mind. Unbidden, unwelcome, it sent the barriers he had built up crashing. His breath caught in his throat and his hand involuntarily jerked the reins so his mare responding to the signal came to a stop. Impatiently he urged her on, trying to crush the unwanted image, obliterate it from his mind. Now, *this minute*. But it persisted, burning brightly in his mind's eye.

A girl's laughing face, head thrown up, beautiful swan's neck, skin like polished ivory, a glorious mane of hair the colour of brandy, thick and wavy, exotic cat's eyes set at a slant, *pure amber*, wide tilted mouth, pointed chin.

Alexandra!

His beautiful, traitorous Alex. The girl who had filled him with such passion he could scarcely live with the thrill of it. The girl who had shared his very soul. He had marvelled at the thread of destiny that had brought them together. He had asked Alex to become his wife, mistress of Main Royal.

God, what a fool! Like his mother, Alex had gone off, following her own star. Alex had wanted it all ways. Marriage and a career. Private and public adulation.

Alexandra Ashton. Nowadays brilliant principal dancer of the Australian Ballet, with rave reviews from Sydney to Moscow. Well, she could dance until she dropped. He never wanted her in his life or on his land again. He had learned to live with her rejection. Only sometimes, like now, the ache was as fierce as an amputation.

He had known Alex since she was ten years old. That was the trouble. She had been so deeply entrenched in his life. Alex too had known tragedy. Her parents had been killed in a terrible six-car pile-up on the state's main highway. It was then Alex had come to Main Royal, a heartbroken little girl. Wyn, as her mother's dearest friend and Alex's godmother, had been appointed guardian in their will, in the event, however remote, that anything should happen to them. He had been seventeen when Alex came to Main Royal. Absurd to fall in love with a *child* but Alex had always been special. A magical creature, with her beautiful colouring and triangular face.

McLaren clenched his jaw and steadfastly pushed the image away from him. It was the only way he could maintain his facade of indifference. It was hard on Wyn loving Alex as she did, but when it came down to it Wyn loved him more. Both of them understood there was only *one* subject in the world they had to avoid even when Alexandra's bright shadow walked between them.

It was dark by the time he and Abe reached the main compound. McLaren bade Abe goodnight, had a word with his overseer about what he required the next day, then walked up to the homestead. The lights from within gleamed golden, spilling out onto the wide verandas that surrounded the house on three sides. Main Royal homestead was a single-storey building but it had been built on the grand scale by his great-grandfather, the Scotsman, Colonel Andrew McLaren, one of the earliest settlers in the state, after a long, distinguished military career.

The verandas alone were a masterpiece in design and construction, the whole architectural concept strongly influenced by the Colonel's years in India with his father who was then the commanding officer of the 75th Regiment. Guest wings had been added in his grandfather's time, carefully in keeping with the design of the main house, and a magnificent ballroom, enclosing the original rear courtyard added for his parents' legendary wedding reception. Main Royal wasn't only a homestead. It was his castle and the ancestral home of the far-flung McLaren clan. Between the uncles, aunts and cousins, the McLarens presided over a pastoral empire.

The double front doors gave onto a spacious parqueted entrance hall with the main reception rooms opening off to left and right. On the circular rosewood library table that stood beneath the splendid Waterford chandelier, Wyn had arranged another magnificent floral display, using all the resources of the five-acre home gardens watered by bores. The arrangements were changed every other day, each seemingly more beautiful than the last. Wyn was a creative artist in more ways than one.

He went straight to his room, showering and changing before he found himself a nice ice-cold beer. His mind should have been on the many issues to hand. He had a speech to write for an industry dinner given in honour of the newly elected state Premier, but thoughts of Alex continued to invade his mind. It was almost as though she was trying to connect with him. Like the old days when their communication had been little short of telepathic.

Wyn had scrapbooks filled with Alex's achievements. Of course he knew where she kept them. He had even in moments of weakness stolen glances at the many glossy photographs of Alexandra Ashton in her many roles—Swan Princess, Sleeping Beauty, Cinderella, Coppelia. Alex leaping free of gravity. Alex in arabesque, turning, *en pointe*. Others (he hated) showing her smiling radiantly at a partner. She always looked marvellously ethereal, a creature of lightness, movement, poetry and magic. No one who could possibly withstand the rigours of station life with the long, savage periods of extreme heat and drought.

It was Wyn ironically who had insisted Alex continue with her ballet lessons. Even as a child she had been incredibly gifted. Her life had to be organised, filled with pursuits that would leave her little time to make herself ill with grief. After a period of adjustment, Alex had gone away to boarding school in Sydney where he too was studying, taking his degree in law. Not that it was ever intended he would practice. The reasoning was that McLaren commercial interests were so vast, legal training could only stand him in good stead and benefit the family interests.

During those years he had picked Alex up at her boarding school every "free day" to take her on some jaunt with one of his numerous girlfriends in tow. Company he called it. One of his girlfriends had suggested with wry humour that chaperone might better cover it. Every vacation Alex spent at the station where she learned to ride like the wind, sleep under the stars, muster and cut cattle, handle a firearm. She loved the life. Adored the space and freedom. So she *said*. She had such a way with her she had charmed every last man, woman and child on the station. Even Abe, the wise, had been her instant slave.

He drank a cold beer from the fridge, poured another into a silver mug and went in search of Wyn. Funny she wasn't around. She usually appeared every time he came back to the house.

He found her behind the desk in her book-lined study, head bent, one hand shielding her forehead.

"Not still working, Wyn?" he asked, moving farther into the wonderfully inviting room and sinking onto one of the leather sofas. She didn't answer immediately and he turned his head in surprise. "Wyn?"

"Sorry, dear."

Her voice sounded husky, as if she'd been crying. Not *Wyn*. Not *crying*. McLaren rose immediately, setting the silver mug down on the low coffee table.

"Wyn, what's the matter?"

The calm, elegant face with the classic McLaren features had a stunned, upset look to it. Worse, little runnels of tears had left their mark on her lightly powdered cheeks.

"What is it? Tell me!" His voice echoed his concern.

Wyn's eyes moved sadly over her nephew's marvellous face. Like his father before him, he was all McLaren, very tall and rangy, with the same look of high mettle, even arrogance and fine breeding. His features were chiselled to perfection, the McLaren cleft in his chin, his fine-grained skin darkly bronzed by the sun. Only the eyes bore witness to Stephanie. They were a wonderful glittering aquamarine. She had never seen such beautiful eyes unless they were...

Alexandra's.

"You're not ill?" McLaren gave his aunt a disturbed glance.

She touched a hand to her hair, once as black as his own, now at sixty pepper-and-salt. "No, dear. It's not that. Not something you'll want to hear, either."

"It's Alex? Isn't it?" he asked abruptly, his striking face clouding over.

"Yes, it's Alex," Wyn sighed, not surprised either by his intuition or reaction. "She's had an accident."

"Accident?" That didn't make him happy. He never wanted Alex harmed.

"It's all here in the paper." Wyn rose stiffly from her chair, newspaper in hand.

"Here, give it to me." His vibrant voice sounded unnaturally harsh. Long-suppressed feelings welled up in him.

"It was during rehearsal," Wyn went on. "That spectacular fish dive at the end of *Aurora* when her partner has to catch her inches from the floor."

"God, you're not going to tell me he *dropped* her?" His voice cracked with anger.

"She took a bad fall. It's all there." Wyn waved a distracted hand. "So cruel. All the work, the sacrifice. It may be gone. Oh, darling, I'm sorry." She turned to him, her heart dropping like a stone at his expression.

"It's all right." His handsome mouth was cool and hard. "It says here she may not dance again." He glanced up at the date. "This paper's a day old."

"Yes. Ed flew in late afternoon." She referred to the pilot of the air freight company they used for their mail and supplies.

"At least you have the name of the hospital they took her to. It says she's expected to undergo surgery. Probably it's already happened."

"My poor little Alex," Wyn moaned.

"She hasn't contacted you?"

"No. She knows..." Wyn faltered and broke off.

"Any mention of her is taboo."

"She knows how much she hurt you, Scott."

"Well, I'm over it." The aqua eyes were like jewels. "I was over it the moment she left."

"She did love you. *Does* love you," Wyn was moved to say.

"Don't break me up." His resonant voice rasped. "All Alex wanted was a brilliant career. To reach the top at any cost. Fair enough. She's had all the attention any young dancer could possibly crave. What we had wasn't *real*. It was more like a dream. An impossible dream. It could never have worked out. Now I finally know it."

"I always thought you were destined for each other." Wyn looked down at her ringless hands.

"You're a hopeless romantic, Wyn."

"I know."

"You want to go to her, don't you?"

"She has no one to turn to, Scotty. You know that."

"Hell, by now she'd have had a dozen lovers," he said with extravagant sarcasm. "A fascinating creature like Alex."

"You don't believe that, surely?" Wyn looked shocked.

"I understood the world of dance was packed with sex," he countered bluntly.

"Alex is the *last* young woman to be promiscuous," Wyn said with certainty. "Her feelings go deep."

He half swung away from her, his body angled so one wide shoulder was higher than the other. "I'm sorry, Wyn, I don't believe that. I don't even care. But I do care about you. If you want to go, you must. I'll arrange it."

Wyn moved towards him and kissed him on the cheek. Tall herself, she had to reach quite a way. "Your heart has always been in the right place. I can see her in hospital, of course. But there's no one to *care* for her, Scotty. Afterwards, I mean. She'll need time to recuperate. She must be mentally and emotionally devastated, as well.''

"You surely can't be asking for her to come *here*?" he asked in a dangerously soft voice.

"She *wouldn't*. She knows you would be very much against it.''

"Why shouldn't I be, Wyn?" He stood quite still, facing her. "She walked out on me. Remember?''

"Scott, she needed you *and* a career. She needed both. She was young. So wonderfully gifted. You have such understanding in every other matter.''

"Not of rejection, I don't,'' he clipped off.

"Your mother did that to you.''

"Leave Stephanie out of it, Wyn,'' he said tonelessly, but she knew not to go further.

"I'm sorry. I'm just so upset.''

"I realise that, Wyn.'' His expression softened. "You're Alex's godmother. You were her guardian until she turned twenty-one. You *love* her despite the fact she almost wrecked my life.''

Wyn's grey eyes were stinging and colour stained her cheeks. "I love *you* more than anyone on earth but I can't lose that sense of responsibility for Alex. I know your love turned to ashes. I know she did everything in her extraordinary power to make you love her. She let you believe your love story was one without end. But she was so *young*. Just nineteen. On the threshold of real achievement. She thought she could have it all. She thought you would support her.''

"From over a thousand miles away?" His tone was taut with derision. "My *wife*, the woman I was crazy for based in Sydney while I was stuck *here*. Young or not, did she really think that would work? That I would be content to let her go? God knows I couldn't go to her. Oh, leave it, Wyn. It's all over and better so. The moment Alex's name crops up our world becomes disruptive. Go if you must. I understand. You can even stay until such time as she can do without you. That's if you believe she's not living with some poor love-struck fool. Just leave me out of it.''

She invaded his dreams. The first time in a long time. He tossed and turned restlessly, getting little much needed sleep. He was still up in the predawn eating a light, solitary breakfast of coffee and toast in the kitchen. Usually he returned to the homestead around eight when Ella, their housekeeper for over twenty years, had something a whole lot more substantial waiting for him. His days were long and hard, from dawn to dusk. He knew he drove himself. He also knew he had to make time and space for a little relaxation and pleasure. He briefly considered his social life. There was always polo, which he loved and excelled at. There were women in his life. Plenty of them for a while. He had done everything he could think of to get over his passion for Alex. Sex without love. To his mind, obviously *one* track, it didn't amount to much. Valerie Freeman was the current woman in his life. Valerie understood him better than most. She was one of the polo set, a glamorous statuesque blonde. One who didn't work because she took a handsome allowance from her grazier father instead. He didn't want to examine his relationship with Valerie too closely. She was good company, good in bed and she didn't cling.

When Wyn walked into the breakfast room, he was horrified by the gauntness of her expression. He rose immediately to draw out a chair for her. ''You had a bad night. Here, let me pour you a cup of tea.'' He walked to the sideboard with its selection of covered dishes.

"I wish *you'd* go, Scott," Wyn burst out without pre-amble, but he knew what she meant.

"For the love of God!" He exhaled a long, weary sigh.

Wyn stared at him for a moment, realising his feelings but unable to cope with her own. She'd had a poor night's sleep and her head was throbbing. "I know we all make too many demands on you," she said emotionally, "but only *you* could persuade Alex to come back. Main Royal belongs to *you*. I can't stay in Sydney indefinitely. I have a deadline to meet."

McLaren poured the tea in silence, put it down before his aunt, then resumed his seat. "Wyn, I'd do anything for you. You know that. You're my favourite person. But to go to Alex. To see her. Speak to her. Invite her to come back to Main Royal. It simply wouldn't work."

"You've never loved anyone else, Scotty," Wyn offered.

"It so happens I find Valerie very attractive," he drawled.

"She's certainly lasted longer than the others." Wyn had to smile, beguiled as ever by the myriad nuances in his voice and expression. "But she hasn't touched your heart. I know you too well, Scotty."

"Then why are you asking me to see Alex?" he challenged.

"Because no one watched over her better than you," she said with remembered pride. "Alex's career could be over. For a normal person the knee would heal and she could get on with life, but *terrible* demands are placed on a dancer. Alex wouldn't be the first to have her career ruined through injury."

Pity stirred deep inside him and something else he didn't want to define. "Even if that were so and I would never wish such a thing on her, how could you possibly imagine we could pick up where we left off? Alex isn't the girl she was. She's a leading ballerina with all the attention that goes with it. She's a glittering creature of the theatre. Anyway, it's not in *me*, Wyn.'' His voice took on a hard edge. ''No woman makes a fool of me. *Twice*.''

Wyn turned her head away abruptly, looking out over the blossoming bauhinias, pink, white and cerise, the flowers as exotic as orchids. ''I was in love once,'' she murmured in a voice that suggested she was talking to herself. ''Even at sixty I've never forgotten.''

''Not the fortune-hunter?'' McLaren asked with the merest lick of cynicism. Everyone in the family knew of Wyn's blighted love affair.

''Father seemed to think so.'' Wyn could remember the misery of it all. ''To Father *and* Mother to a much lesser extent—she liked him but she never would go against Father—he was a charming rogue.''

''But wasn't he, Wyn?'' McLaren asked very gently.

Wyn's fine grey eyes looked sad. ''He was penniless certainly. Adventuring his way around the world. But I truly believe he loved me.''

McLaren rose and rested his hand on his aunt's shoulder. ''Then I'm sure he did, Wyn. You're a beautiful woman. Inside and out.''

''He's *Someone* now,'' Wyn added with a faintly ironic smile.

McLaren looked at her in surprise. ''I've never heard anything of it.''

Wyn shrugged. ''He changed his name. Grew rather a distinguished beard. I knew him all the same. I'd know him anywhere.''

McLaren was intrigued, aquamarine eyes gleaming. ''So are you going to tell me?''

''Better forgotten, darling,'' Wyn said lightly. ''He

wouldn't want to remember me or my family. All we did was cause him pain and humiliation. Father literally ran him off the station. Put the word out he was a scoundrel.''

McLaren's mouth was wry. "He was a pretty terrifying old guy, Grandad."

"Yes," Wyn sighed. "But he loved me. He believed he was doing the right thing. Anyway, who knows? Father might have been right. Still, he must have cared for me because he sent me a dozen letters or more after that. Mama didn't hand them over until Father died. I was a few years short of fifty. Can you believe it?''

McLaren's handsome face turned sardonic. "Knowing my grandparents, yes. You're not bitter, Wyn?" he said, thinking she had cause to be.

Wyn looked up to smile at him. "No, darling. Father thought he was acting responsibly. If I'd had the courage I could have gone with him. I didn't. I was expected to marry Grant McEwan, as you know. Everyone thought it would happen, especially poor Grant. I'd come to my senses. I never did."

McLaren's vibrant voice held a tender note. "I'm sorry, Wyn. I truly am. You're one track. Like *me*."

It was an admission of sorts. "Does that mean you'll go to Alex?" Wyn asked hopefully, her heart in her eyes.

McLaren moved restlessly, tension in his lean body, his face betraying the memory of hollow longing. "I'll go, Wyn, if only to set *your* mind at rest. At this stage I only intend to check on Alex's well-being. But I'll never forgive her. *Ever*. Unlike you, I'm as bitter as hell."

CHAPTER TWO

THE receptionist peered through the sliding glass window, her severe face brightening into a smile. "Good morning. May I help you?"

He returned the smile briefly, his nerves stretched taut. "You have an Alexandra Ashton as a patient, orthopaedic ward, I would think."

"Miss Ashton, of course," she said without hesitation. "We won't need the computer to give you the ward number and room. The hospital has been besieged by calls ever since she was admitted. So beautiful and so popular. I've attended many of her performances. Family or friend?"

"Family," he half lied. What *was* Alex these days?

"I'm sure she'll be *thrilled* to see you," the woman gushed. "Ward 5, Room 16. Do you know your way?"

For a moment it looked as if she was about to leave her work station. "Thank you," he said briskly, starting to move off. "I'll find it."

It was a big hospital but he located the ward without trouble, walking down the corridors with his long stride. Groups of people huddled in the waiting rooms, stared out at him as he walked past. Hell, what am I, the man from Mars? he thought irritably, when the truth was that never in his life would he go unnoticed.

As he approached Room 16, he slowed, willing himself back to control. Three years since he'd last seen Alex. Three years since she had finally left him to start her new life. It only seemed like yesterday with all yesterday's torment.

Three women manned the nurses' station, taking time out to give him a thorough inspection. He nodded briefly in their direction and turned into Room 16 where the door lay open. Beautiful flower arrangements stood on every available free surface—roses, orchids, lilies, magnificent pink and white carnations in a beribboned white basket—all spreading their fragrance, but he barely registered them. His whole attention was given over to the young woman in the bed. Superbly fit, he was momentarily weakened by the old sense of loss. It tore at him, so for a brief moment he felt like turning on his heel and walking away—right out of the hospital.

The things Wyn asked him to do. But hadn't he wanted it himself? He couldn't ignore the fact even if he knew coming here was a mistake.

Her head was turned away from him towards the window with its slanting rays of sunlight, her masses of hair confined at the nape—a rich golden brown, cognac? amber? anyway, an indescribable colour and one that could never be duplicated from a bottle. It made a bright splash of colour against the white pillows. Her legs were hidden beneath the bed covers but her upper body was exposed. She was wearing one of her own nightgowns, a delicate garment adorned with the usual feminine fripperies of ribbons and lace. She was so slight. *Too* slight. Probably anorexic, her slender arms arranged, even now, in an innately graceful pose.

Was she sleeping?

He approached her with his soundless tread and as he did so she turned her head swiftly, her huge eyes betraying shock, perhaps premonition. Another one of her little tricks.

"Scott!"

Incredibly he wanted to reach out for her, gather her

up, mould her body to him as he had done countless times before.

God, what a fool! *Deal with it*, he thought. Deal with it. She walked out on you, remember?

He gave himself time before he spoke. "Hello, Alex," he said carefully, little realising his eyes reflected a hard brilliance. "I hope I didn't startle you?"

She shook her head though she could feel shock waves vibrating through her body. It seemed like a *miracle*! To wish for him and he was there. Spontaneously she extended her hand. "I was only thinking of you. Can you *believe* that?"

He said nothing but his handsome mouth compressed. He didn't *want* to take that graceful white hand. It was too damn hard not to. "I'm sorry about your accident, Alex." The struggle for control left his voice harsh. "What exactly *is* wrong?" Sensation slashed at him as their skin made contact. Her hand was so small and fragile in his grasp, cool yet burning.

"It's complicated, Scott." Her voice was more subdued now as the full extent of their rift became apparent. She was uncomfortably aware he hadn't wanted to touch her. "It comes under the general heading of collateral ligament injuries. A severe rupture in my case. It requires surgical treatment."

"You haven't had it as yet?" He glanced down at the outline of her legs, so slight beneath the covers.

"No. It's scheduled for tomorrow morning. Nine-thirty a.m. They wanted to build me up a little first."

His lips moved in a tense smile. The smile she hoped for was never going to come. "You look as though the breeze could blow you away."

"I've had to keep as light as possible," she admitted. "Part of the price. I admit I've come close to exhaustion. Touring takes it out of one. Please sit down." She indicated an armchair. "You're so *tall*." So vivid, so vital, so heart-stoppingly handsome his presence filled the room; made the very air vibrate.

Now he reached for a chair, twisting it closer to the bed. "Wyn sends her love," he said, settling his lean frame. "She read about your accident in the newspaper and showed it to me. Naturally she's very upset."

Alex lowered her head, casting around for the right thing to say. "Wyn always loved and stood by me. Even through the mess I made of things. *I am so sorry*."

"Ancient history, Alex," he said in a clipped voice. "What happened happened and that's the end of it."

"But it leaves a scar, doesn't it?" She lifted her amber eyes to him.

"That's the way life is." He shrugged. "Some relationships inflict more damage than others. The important thing is in *our* case we recognised it would never work. So what's the prognosis?" He switched the subject deliberately. "It must be causing you a great deal of anxiety."

"It's quite possible I'll never dance again," she answered simply. It was true but not the crushing blow it might once have been.

"That must be hard to take." He kept all trace of bitterness out of his voice. Enchantress that she was, all the old protective feelings had come rushing back the moment he saw her.

"It's all I know." She tried to keep the strain from her voice but it showed.

"Who's to do the operation?" he asked, more upset by the sight of her than he wanted or needed. "A good man, I hope."

"The best." Her heavily lashed eyes swept like butterfly wings all over his face.

She had a frightening power had Alex.

"Am I going to hear his name?" He spoke as though he had little taste for her magic.

"Of course," she sighed in wry acknowledgment. "Ian Tomlinson," she told him. "He's the top orthopaedic surgeon in the country. I'm lucky. He's only just returned from a six-month stint in Canada. He assured me he's going to do his very best for me, but I'm not to get my hopes up I can return to my career."

"Perhaps you'll prove him wrong." He felt compelled to comfort her. "Are you in a lot of pain?" Her eyes were like saucers, swamping her triangular face. She was extremely pale, too, her beautiful skin and sensitive mouth innocent of make-up. He had never thought she needed it anyway.

"They bring me something every few hours. I've learned to live with pain, Scott."

"That makes two of us," he said laconically. "Where are your friends, or do they just send flowers?" Only now did he look around him, studying the exquisite and obviously very expensive floral arrangements. He caught himself before he made a move to read the cards.

"They call in from time to time," Alex explained. "I'm not lonely. The company will be moving to Adelaide at the end of the week for the festival."

"Anyone in particular you need to see?"

Her lashes swept down protectively. She didn't want him to see the vulnerability reflected in her eyes. He was so achingly handsome, his natural *presence* more marked with maturity. The air still crackled around him, his eyes sparkled just as brilliantly, but the vivid mobility of his expression had been replaced by a daunting air of command. "There's no man in my life, Scott. If that's what you mean."

There was scepticism in his gaze. "Forgive me if I find that very hard to believe."

"It's true all the same. There's never much time in my life for anything else but work. I am—*was*—one of the determined ones."

"You don't have to tell me." He stared right back at her.

She tilted her head, showing the long, graceful line of her throat. "How have *you* been?" she asked. "And Wyn? I miss her so much."

"Fine," he answered in a sardonic voice. "We're both well. Wyn is still writing her stories. Her publisher can't get enough of them. The illustrations, I always think, are a marvellous selling point."

"Magic." Alex smiled for the first time.

The beautiful gold flecks were still in her eyes; her mouth curled up enchantingly. Alex the exquisite little cat with the sheathed claws...

"You're selfish!" she had hurled at him, her graceful body seemingly so fragile, yet so wonderfully strong and springy, trembling with outrage. "It's all about *you*. *Your* Dream. *Your* Quest. What *you* want. The splendid Scott McLaren, lord of a million acres, master of Main Royal. You want to *own* me. You want to deny me my chance. Well, I refuse to toe your line. I won't have it. Do you hear?"

He had heard all right. She'd always had a temper, an inner fire, but he'd never heard her so assertive, so set on being independent. Now when she had him deeply in love with her, crazy to marry her, he discovered to his cost she had made *her* crucial choice. She wanted to push her career to the limits. She wanted to *make* it before she settled down. Husband and family were her *long*-term goals. In the meantime he would have to be content with lengthy periods of separation.

What a fool he had been. He had never realised she was so focused, so ambitious. He thought they had *shared* all their feelings, but she had remained silent, quietly working out her own agenda. Women were devious. Not like men. Women betrayed trust. When it came down to it, much as she protested she loved him, she placed her career foremost in life.

For his part he hadn't left her to assume anything. Growing up as she had on Main Royal, Alex knew as well as he the station was a total commitment. He couldn't walk away from it short of abdicating his inheritance and his responsibilities to the McLaren clan with their diversity of interests. Alex knew that. She'd always known it. He thought she had accepted it. Only on the eve of their engagement did she make it clear she wanted a foot in both worlds.

Well, it wouldn't work. He *needed* her not only for the physical passion they shared but for all happiness and purpose in life. *She* was the integral part of his Dream. Alex needed something else. He'd had to face that squarely.

"What are you thinking about?" she asked as the silence grew uncomfortably long.

It took him a moment to respond. "If you must know, I was lost in memory."

"Not pleasant by the expression on your face."

"No," he said dismissively, looking past her to the door. "Time, I think, for your medication."

A stocky, pleasant-faced nurse bustled in, speaking cheerfully to Alex as though she were a child.

"Here we are, love." She passed a capsule, then a paper cup of water. "Swallow it down like a good girl." While she spoke she was studying McLaren avidly across the bed, thinking she had never seen such a stunning-looking man in her whole life. Those *eyes*. The colour! Not that the atmosphere inside the room could possibly be described as lovey-dovey. It was emotional certainly, but crackling with electricity. "Push the button if you need me," she found herself saying to her patient as she walked to the door.

"What the devil was that about?" McLaren asked with muted irony after the nurse had disappeared. "Call if you *need* me? Am I supposed to be some sort of a threat?"

"I suppose she thought the air was thick with tension," Alex offered wryly. "You look much more formidable than you used to. In fact, you haven't smiled once since you walked in the door."

"Surely there's nothing much to smile about," he countered. "It doesn't make me happy to see you with serious injuries and in pain."

She waited to collect herself. "One of the many reasons I loved you," she said gently. "You pick up on people's pain. You *care*. That's why everyone on the station blesses your name."

"You were pretty popular yourself. *Once*," he pointed out coolly.

"I do realise I'll never be forgiven."

"Shocking, but true." He nodded and leaned back. "Anyway, I didn't come here to rake up the past, though I don't believe any of us can banish it at will. Wyn and I are *concerned* about you. It's impossible to forget what you meant to us. Have you anyone to look after you when you come out of hospital? You'll be in plaster, won't you? Possibly for up to eight weeks?"

"Yes."

He stared back at her. A firebird. Grounded.

"Six weeks if I'm lucky." There was no self-pity in her tone. "I'll be fine, Scott. There's no need for *Wyn* to worry about me."

His extraordinary eyes narrowed. "You haven't

changed. I'd expect you to say that. So who is this person or persons you can turn to?''

In reality she was very much on her own. Especially with the company on tour. Her whole world was the ballet, her friends other dancers all fully committed to a tight schedule. "I can get someone in," she said without hesitation, pride and a terrible longing for him warring within her.

He seemed to tense. "You might consider Wyn is anxious to discharge what she considers her sacred duty. Your parents appointed her to care for you. The caring didn't stop when you ran off. She's been very much affected by our estrangement.''

She gave a small, almost helpless shrug. "I write to her as often as I can.''

"And she writes back to you. It's no big secret. You didn't let her know about your fall however.''

"I didn't want to upset her," Alex said with perfect truth. "I didn't think the newspapers would report it, much less at such length.''

"My dear Alexandra." His tone was dry. "You're famous. Why *wouldn't* they report it?''

She said nothing, obviously not realising she was so newsworthy. "And Wyn showed it to you?''

"Surely you didn't think I'd get any satisfaction from it? I'm no sadist," he retorted, shoving a hand through his thick, jet black hair.

"Of course not," she hurried to placate him, "but I know you wanted to break all connection with me.''

"Pardon me, Alex. It was the *other* way around," he said coldly. *You* were the one who wanted your brilliant career. You could hardly expect any man worth his salt to let his new bride out of his sight. Maybe it's different with you women. You seem to be able to turn it on and off at will.''

She swallowed on a hard lump in her throat. "I loved you, Scott, with all my heart."

He felt a surge of anger but quickly repressed it. "Alex, you don't even know the meaning of the word. Perhaps you decided as a bereaved little girl never to give your heart again. Loving is loss. Loving is dangerous. It puts one at risk. If you don't love you can't get hurt. The way out is to have someone else do the loving. There's always one who kisses and one who turns the cheek."

Alex looked past his gleaming head to the window. Her sense of loss had deepened through the years she had been away from him just as her memories had become more vivid. She remembered every minute they had spent together; their tremendous empathy, their shared sense of humour. Most of all she remembered the first time he had kissed her, an action that had turned her overnight from little more than a schoolgirl to a yearning woman....

It was the night of her seventeenth birthday. Wyn had arranged a gala ball for her in the Great Hall. People had come from all over the country to attend it: their far-flung Outback neighbours who, living in everyday isolation, adored nothing more than a party, their friends from the cities, the entire McLaren clan. Even Scott's beautiful mother, Stephanie, not averse to these glittering occasions, had secured herself an invitation.

It had been the most magical night. A *triumph*. She truly had been the belle of the ball, dressed in a shimmering dress of topaz silk taffeta with a billowing skirt that swept the floor as she danced. There had been many young men that night, handsome, virile, all highly eligible, but Scott had drawn the eye like flame. Her heart had rocked in her breast at the first sight of him in evening dress. To put it simply, she was spellbound and spellbound she remained. From the first day she had come to Main Royal, Scott had treated her like a cherished little cousin. He had been endlessly kind, understanding, indulgent. Only very occasionally had he shown steel when she tried to overstep the limits of personal safety he had set her. Of course, he had always been right, but she secretly enjoyed those little clashes, tilting at his lordly position, pushing his patience to the very edge.

That night, he had been surrounded by the usual bevy of adoring females all mad with longing to have Scott pay them some attention. He was and remained an outstanding catch. A *dream* of a man! Handsome, brilliant, rich. Some of the polo set were only interested in rich beaux and not ashamed to admit it, either. Scott McLaren had it all.

As she looked at all those pretty, eager faces, she remembered she had felt an emotion that was as new as it was painful. It twisted and coiled inside her, so just to get rid of it, she did something completely out of character. She began flirting outrageously with each partner in turn. She was overwhelmed by a mix of emotions that made her feel giddy. Too many extravagant compliments were being paid to her. Finally Scott stood beside her, apparently none too pleased with her seductive behaviour or the way her partner of the moment was holding her. Much too *tightly*. Knowing Scott as well as she did, she could tell his every mood from the glitter of his eyes, a certain angle of his handsome head, the faint jut of his cleft chin.

He looked down at her partner, smiled very coolly, then swooped her up and moved into an old swing waltz an older member of the family had requested while the young ones joined in with an enthusiasm that made up for their lack of expertise. Her beautiful Scott, so superbly coordinated with a natural rhythm in every muscle of his body had never missed a beat although it wasn't what he was used to, either. As a trained dancer, she slipped into any style easily, weightless in his arms. She knew he didn't want to spoil her magical night just as she knew he was concerned to curb her little excesses.

"Did I tell you how beautiful you look tonight?" he said in a voice that left her shaking and breathless. She was positive he had never used such a voice to her before.

"No, you didn't," she answered, covering her confusion with a bright smile. "You *never* tell me I'm beautiful. In fact, you never compliment me on my looks."

"I might have to start now you're growing up," he said with a kind of self-mockery. "Just one thing. Don't break too many hearts tonight. Most of the guys here you've known all your life. They're friends. I don't want them looking at you in an entirely different light."

"What about *you*?" Incredibly she had said it, her mind and body filled with this perilous new excitement. There was too much music, too much laughter, too many glittering decorations and the perfume of a million flowers. She was totally off balance whirling in Scott's arms.

"I'm the one you're *not* allowed to play games with, remember?"

In other words he was telling her he was quite beyond her reach.

After that there was no reason to behave. She worked herself even more convincingly into the role of Scarlett O'Hara, not doing a bad job of it, either, a talent she was to carry into her dancing. Finally, some time after midnight, Scott caught her hand and propelled her out into the star-filled night, finding a quiet corner where there was no chance of being overheard.

She remembered the purplish black velvet sky. It was

heavily embroidered with jewels, a billion white diamonds intermingled with the ruby and sapphire glitter of the stars that sent out more light energy. The starlight *blazed* as only it can over the desert.

"For God's sake, Alex," Scott demanded, taking her by the arms and turning her to face him. "What are you trying to do?"

Make you look at me. Wasn't that the whole truth of it? Instead, she answered quite flippantly, "I'm sure I don't know what you mean."

He wasn't about to be fooled or fobbed off. "Don't give me that," he bluntly contradicted her. "I'm only trying to protect you. Surely you know that. You can sparkle all you like. This is *your* ball, *your* special night, but clearly you're having one hell of an effect. How does a girl go from sweet sixteen to a temptress with no preparation?"

"Easy," she sweetly mocked. "Yesterday I was a child. Tonight I'm a *woman*. What's wrong with that?"

"You want the truth?" He sounded faintly goaded. "You're not a woman. *Yet*."

How *that* had stung!

"Every man at the ball seems to think so," she taunted him. "Everyone but *you*."

Recklessly she swayed towards him, emotions vacillating madly inside her. She remembered how his hands came up to grasp her bare shoulders; she remembered his warm breath on her cheek before he pulled her to him, hurting her a little when she knew he never meant to. "Tonight *anyone* could make you feel like a woman. I'll prove it."

The stars had fallen from the sky, landing like fiery flowers all around them.

The first touch of his mouth filled her with such yearning it was almost despair. How foolish she had been to tempt him. The kiss went on and on until even Scott seemed to be struggling to stem the tide of passion neither of them had counted on. She had been trembling so badly she was afraid she wouldn't be able to go back into the hall. Every shred of pride, of self-control, of dignity, was threatened. She would live with that moment forever; the blinding shock of it, the exquisite flood of sensation that ravished her. Why, they were practically *cousins*! She had tagged after Scott since she was ten years old. She *loved* him. She'd loved him from day one when he'd held a sobbing little girl in his arms. He was her *hero*. She hadn't counted on falling deeply, crazily, *in* love. She hadn't counted on this sweep-all-before-it sensuality.

After that she had wanted him so badly it hurt. She had laughed at it, wept with it; tried desperately to live with it, learn from it.

"I'm not the only one who's getting lost in the past."

Scott's voice so deep and sardonic brought her back to the present. Only one voice like Scott's, only one voice to make her heart beat in her ears.

"The fact is I think of you often," she said with a sort of sadness. Every instinct told her he didn't want to hear it.

"Then I hope you *cry*," he said softly, only she saw the shimmering bitterness in his eyes.

"Maybe I do." She gave a wry smile. "I didn't get by without punishment. Thank you for coming to see me, Scott. Thank you for caring enough."

His bronze face immediately emptied of expression. "I'd be less than human if I didn't. And there was Wyn. She was deeply upset at the news."

Both of them grew quiet, then Alex asked, "Did you fly yourself in?"

"Of course." He was quite matter-of-fact, as used to

piloting light aircraft and helicopters as driving any station vehicle.

"I hope you could spare the time." Most days were planned. Scott worked very hard.

He shrugged. "Wyn was in a state of agitation bordering on hysteria. She loves you dearly. To her you'll always be family. She was concerned about the psychological effects, as well. In fact, she asked me to convey to you her dearest wish you'll recuperate on Main Royal."

For an instant it took her breath away. Lovely Wyn!

"But *you* don't want me." She sobered up.

"My dear Alex, so much time has passed I don't *care*." His tone was acid. "What little spare time I have, I think we can manage to get on. You won't be able to do much but lie around. Besides, I have business in Japan next month. I should have remembered to tell you Ella sends her love." He referred to Main Royal's housekeeper who had been such a friend to the young Alex. "Ella would like nothing better than to cosset you."

Behind the smooth exterior, Alex could sense the flickering steel in him. He was *sorry* for her but he didn't want her around him. What they had could start up again. The chemistry between them had been just that strong. *Tyrannical*.

Alex bent her head, looking down at her entwined hands. Sometimes it even struck *her* how her every gesture was unconsciously balletic. Look at her hands now! Who did she think she was? Juliet? She glanced up quickly at Scott only to see an answering ironic awareness in his eyes. She hadn't planned on being a ballerina. Showing Scott she could be *Someone* was part of it.

"I'm deeply grateful to Wyn and Ella for wanting me," she told him. "I'll be writing to Wyn just as soon as I can, but you and I know it would never work. There's just too much history between us.''

"You could be kidding yourself," he drawled, lounging back gracefully. "Life moves on, Alex. Though I can't deny your rejection hurt at the time, you've been replaced.''

Silence.

Finally she spoke. "Of course. There would be hundreds to pick from.''

"Valerie Freeman," he said with a cool smile. "You remember Valerie?''

"The tall blonde?" Valerie of the polo set with a phenomenally rich father.

"I can't see enough of her," Scott confessed. "What about you? You say there's no one when we both know your way with men is miraculous.''

"I'm heart free." She kept her voice light, not wanting him to know how he hurt her. No one but Scott had ever meant anything.

"Amazing, if one were to believe all the gossip," he mocked.

"What gossip?" There was a momentary flash in her amber eyes.

"Wasn't there the guy who looked a bit like Baryshnikov? On and offstage chemistry, wasn't it? I occasionally see Wyn's clippings.''

"All PR," she said. No point whatever in mentioning the mesmeric Victor was gay.

"I'll stay on tomorrow until you're through the operation," he said, careless of her answer as though he believed she was lying.

"You don't have to do that, Scott." She shook her head, holding on to her pride.

"It's *settled*." He looked and sounded inflexible. "We'll keep in touch until you're ready to be discharged. "I should be able to pick you up here at the hospital and fly you back to the station. You can let us know your therapy once you come out of plaster. We have the pool and we can get a physiotherapist to live in. I'm sure there's someone."

It was like the old days when everything was decided. "I appreciate this, Scott," she said a little tautly, "but I don't feel I can take you up on your very generous offer. I truly *do* have people to look out for me. I have my own doctor. His surgery is down the street. There are nurses who call. Hiring a physiotherapist to come all the way out to Main Royal would be a very big expense."

"Alex, I can supply you with anything you want," he said shortly.

Of course! The McLarens had so much money they never talked about it. He could supply her with everything *material*, but the old days were long gone. She may not have broken his heart but she had damaged his pride. Scott McLaren was a proud man.

"Let me think it over," she suggested, her thoughts in some turmoil. One part of her longed to return to Main Royal; the other was deeply conscious of the fact Wyn had put pressure on him to come here. Even his body language locked her out. She didn't know if she could cope with it or having Valerie Freeman under her nose. The old jealousy was still in place, only this time she had no right to it.

"I think you owe it to Wyn, perhaps?" He spoke coolly, but the hidden rebuke penetrated.

"Maybe I could come out for a short visit when I'm out of plaster."

"You might have nowhere else to go," he said bluntly. "I think you should be with people who care about you."

"I've faced the fact, Scott, I might never dance again." Even so, her voice broke.

"It's been your whole purpose in life."

An incontrovertible fact.

But then he had never truly understood how she felt. She had wanted to *prove* herself as a person. She had wanted to prove *his* match. In retrospect she realised that *that* had been her true ambition. To prove her worth not only to herself but to the man she loved.

Seven years her senior, Scott was already owner of a great station with limitless power in his own kingdom. Scott had seen her need to spread her wings as a total rejection of him; as a wilful determination to breach the castle walls. He'd been madly in love with her, his feelings turbulent. Scott was and always would be a man of strong passions. Having her close to him was an obsession. Though he would never admit it, he had been *afraid* of losing her. Scott McLaren, incomparably brave and daring, *afraid*?

She only saw later that his anxiety flowed deeply from his mother's defection. In some ways, Stephanie represented *all* women. Women who wielded awesome power over their men. She had *insulted* him, just as Stephanie had insulted his beloved father's memory. Scott was complex, a man of wide-ranging emotions. More pertinently, he had been reared in a *man's* world.

While she was agonising, Alex was worrying the ribbon that tied back her hair. Now it began to unfurl, falling like a bright veil of silk around her face and tumbling over her shoulders. Like all classical dancers, she had to keep her hair long. Now it reached halfway down her back.

"How beautiful you are!" he said with supreme detachment. "You have the gift of enchanting the eye. It's nothing less than magic."

She had to curb the flood of emotion that rushed through her; the memory of the times she had rested back in his arms, his hand moving caressingly through her long hair. Ward Sister saved her. She came to the door acknowledging Scott with a smile before speaking to Alex. "Mr Tomlinson is in the hospital, dear. I'm expecting him shortly. Also your anaesthetist, Dr Brownley will be wanting to have a word with you."

Scott rose immediately, six foot three of dynamic male. "Sounds like it's time for me to go."

Alex lay back, staring up at him. "Thank you for coming, Scott." Unexpectedly, *wretchedly*, the tears began. She was weak, in pain and much, much too vulnerable.

There was a swift change in his expression. "You'll make it, Alex," he said in a deep, reassuring voice. "You've got plenty of guts. You'll dance again. I *know* it."

He moved to clasp her hand, looking down at it for a moment before he bent his head to brush a brief kiss on her cheek. A single pearl-shaped tear rolled between his mouth and her skin.

"I'll see you when you come round after the operation," he promised.

"Listen to me, Scott," she began, still clutching his hand. She wasn't even sure what she was going to say to him. That she loved him? That she'd always loved him? That she wanted her time all over again? Nothing in the world of dance could match the incomparable joy she had known with him.

She seemed to be throbbing with pain. A level she had never experienced before. Her mind felt befuddled with all the pain-killing drugs. Her injuries had left her emotionally as well as physically drained. It was brought home to her, too, what true love was all about. She could *never* break the bond that tied her to Scott. All the time she had been away from him, she had never been able to form another *real* relationship. She wanted to tell him that. She wanted to tell him how she had missed him. She wanted to make that very clear. She wanted to *beg* him to stay.

"Scott!" she said again, her eyes betraying her agitation.

"It's all right, Alex." He bent over her, pushing her hair back. There was the most devastating note of concern in his voice even if he misinterpreted the true source of her anguish. "You're in good hands. Your doctor will be along soon. You've always been brave. *I* should know. You'll get through this. I'll be back tomorrow."

Oh please, God, *yes*, she thought, lifting her hand to acknowledge his parting salute. Scott was so strong. He had always had the capacity to make her feel enormously safe and secure.

Only she recognised with a crushing sense of loss that he wasn't *her* Scott any more.

[illegible faint text from previous page showing through]

CHAPTER THREE

HE ARRIVED back at his hotel to find a red light flashing on the bedside console indicating there was a message. Probably Wyn, he thought, throwing off his jacket. She'd be anxious for news though she should have known he'd contact her as soon as he could.

What to tell her? He wasn't at all sure Alex would accept his offer. Alex, the independent, had her own pride. Besides, she had always been able to read his mind. She knew he didn't want her back to overturn his life. Having her on Main Royal would only stir up all the old emotions he'd done his best to bury.

Alex, the firebird, was trouble. Woman magic, Abe would call it. She'd led him a thrilling but ultimately bitter dance. It would pay him to remember it.

He sat down on the side of the bed to ring through to reception, expecting the message to be from Wyn, surprised and oddly not all that delighted to hear it was from Valerie, who had been staying with her aunt and uncle at their Sydney mansion. The message was succinct. RING ME? How the devil did she know he was in Sydney, or at the Hyatt on the Park, for that matter? The only way was that she'd put through a call to Main Royal and Wyn had told her. He wondered if Wyn had given her the reason for his visit. Probably not. Valerie was as keen as he was to relegate Alex to the past.

He made a few calls to family, friends and a couple of business associates before ringing Valerie, suggesting, as he knew she expected, dinner at Pierre's. Valerie was very attractive, good company. Ordinarily he was happy to hear from her, so what was the problem?

Don't ask, he thought grimly, his mind filled with the image of Alex lying so pale and apprehensive in that hospital bed. Three years since she'd fled from him, yet they had bridged the intervening years like so many minutes.

Around seven-thirty when he arrived to pick up Valerie, he found the family assembled in the living room—Valerie's uncle and aunt and Valerie's cousin, Zara, a Valerie look-alike—faces beaming, the atmosphere uncomfortably *expectant*. It was brought home to him forcibly that Valerie and her entire family were hoping for big things from this relationship. Hell, why not? He wasn't seeing anyone else. He was thirty years old. Even *he* knew it was high time he found himself a wife. Main Royal needed an heir. Besides, as an only child, he wanted family. He and Alex had planned on three children. Just another fantasy she had played out.

Heads turned when they entered the restaurant. Valerie looked stunning in sleek black silk that showed off her statuesque figure and one of her best assets, her long, long legs. Her ash blond hair fell in a clean, straight sweep to her shoulders. He liked that. In high heels, she stood almost level with his chin. No flatties for Valerie. No stoop. She carried herself proudly even if he was aware she revelled in *his* height. It wasn't the moment to think of the way Alex had nestled against his heart.

Alex! He should have known the very sight of her would stir up the old torment. But it was over, that other life. He had made a fresh start. A new beginning. Even so, he hadn't been able to bring himself to making a commitment to Valerie. It was unworthy of him and unfair to her. But he hadn't lied to her. He had made no promises. If he wanted to be ungallant, he could say Valerie had made quite a bit of the running, but he had to take full responsibility if the relationship continued much further. He couldn't use Valerie as an emotional crutch. That would be too deplorable.

This business of Alex had to come to an end. She was a real threat to his plans. Recognising her essential toughness, her inner strengths, he knew Alex had the capacity to triumph over this tremendous setback. If anyone could get themselves mobile, it would be Alex. She would mend and take off again. To her world of ballet. That was the really important thing to remember.

For Valerie's part, no one could have been more conscious of the stir they created when they entered the restaurant. She knew she would be the envy of every woman in the room. Scott McLaren really was something else! So gloriously tall and handsome with that innate air of breeding and authority. His late father had carried himself the same way. There was something very special about powerful men. Even her father—and he had lost most of his hair—had a considerable presence. She liked her men not only rich but *achievers*. She saw *her* job as landing one. She had worked very hard on Scott, never giving up hope that one day he would forget the charismatic Alexandra Ashton.

Despite her personal animosity, she had seen Alexandra dance many times, enchanted by the young woman's incredible grace and beauty. It seemed wildly incongruous such an ethereal creature had ever found her way to the Outback. A vast cattle station of all places, sited as it was on the fringe of the desert heart. Like everyone else, Valerie had read in the newspapers about Alexandra's bad fall; seen it on the television, the announcement accompanied by a brief glimpse of her dancing the role of Aurora. She remembered she'd felt a rush of disquiet at the time as though this new development could directly affect her life and interfere in her plans.

She wondered now as she had all day what the exact reason was for Scott's visit to Sydney. She fervently hoped it was to see one of his many business associates or financial advisers. The very last thing in the world she wanted to hear was that he had flown in solely to see Alexandra Ashton. Edwina hadn't told her a thing. But then Edwina wouldn't. Valerie knew perfectly well how she rated with Edwina McLaren.

Over a dry martini, Valerie risked a direct question. As self-confident as she was, she never knew *exactly* where she stood with Scott. He was so darn elusive but so *sexy*! Just the sound of his voice on the telephone was enough to make her go weak at the knees. "So what *really* brought you to Sydney?" She smiled at him, her hazel eyes sending out a challenge. "You're not going to tell me it was to see *me*?"

He laughed, then stroked her hand, increasing the effect of that breathtaking sexuality. "I always want to see you, Val, but this time it was an errand for Wyn."

Valerie felt a sharp twinge of alarm. "It must have been urgent to get you to leave the station."

He gave a slight nod, his eyes drifting away across the serene, romantic room. "I expect you've read about it in the newspapers. Alex had a bad fall. She's in hospital awaiting an operation on her knee."

Alex. Oh no! Valerie picked up her drink, took a quick, calming sip. "I did read about it as a matter of fact. She even made the TV news." Despite herself her voice held a hard note.

"She *is* one of the stars of the Australian Ballet." His brilliant gaze came back to her.

Was it her imagination or was it that least bit *frosty*?

One of the things that disturbed her about Scott was that he could be very touchy about *family*. And that included that little bitch, Alexandra. Just when Valerie thought they were free of her, she'd popped up again.

Valerie willed her facial muscles into an expression of concern. "Of course, and so gifted. I've seen her many times and been enchanted by her performances. Wyn would be tremendously upset. She has such *heart*." Not for *me*, Valerie thought. The patrician Edwina wasn't above a little scheming of her own, either. "So you flew all this way to visit Alex in hospital?"

"Could you think of a *better* way?" He shrugged carelessly.

His compelling voice was as smooth as cream but something in his demeanour stopped her. "And how *is* she?" Valerie enquired solicitously albeit a little late. "She must be terrified her career could be in jeopardy."

"I'm sure she is, but she's keeping herself together. This isn't the first terrible blow Alex has taken."

"So protective still, Scott?" She couldn't control the taunt as her own deep jealousies rose perilously to the surface.

"I can't forget Alex was a long time in my life, Val," he pointed out, his expression thrillingly dark and brooding.

But not for *her*. "I'm sorry, darling." Instantly Valerie reached out, placing her beautifully manicured fingers over his. "You can't blame me for being anxious. I know how much chaos Alex brought to your life. Women like that can be very dangerous."

"Can't they just!" His mouth curved slightly.

It was far from the response Valerie wanted. "Well, if she's unable to resume dancing, she can always marry one of her many admirers," she offered as though perfectly serious. "It's impossible to get near her after a performance. There's been a lot of talk about one of her partners, too. Victor Dreyer. A very good-looking man.''

"I really haven't given the matter much attention.'' He shrugged. "Alex might look fragile but she's very strong. The result of years of intense training. She's a determined person, as well. If it's humanly possible to get back, she will.''

"I really do hope so,'' Valerie said with unfeigned sincerity. "It would be a tragedy for such a brilliant dancer to be robbed of her career. Dancers are tremendously committed people. And she faces an operation?''

"Tomorrow morning.'' McLaren picked up his drink casually. The glow from the tapering candle on the table centre washed his face with gold. "I want to be there to see how it goes.''

"Naturally.'' Valerie swallowed hard on the bitter taste in her mouth. "It's a wonder Wyn didn't come with you. I know how very fond she is of her goddaughter.''

McLaren gave another one of his elegant shrugs. The aura he gave off was incredible. Supercharged. "No real need,'' he said. "Wyn wants Alex to recuperate on Main Royal.''

"*What*?'' Though she could have kicked herself, it came out as a spontaneous near shout.

"Hey, what's the problem?'' McLaren held up a mocking hand. "I didn't particularly *want* this, Val. But I can't have Wyn distressed. Seeing Alex lying in that hospital bed, I wouldn't want her to be without proper care, either.''

"But surely she has *friends*?'' Valerie bit down on her tongue so she wouldn't snap. "There must be scores of people who'd jump at the chance to look after her. Good grief, she's *famous*. I know people myself who would think it quite a coup to have Alexandra Ashton recuperate on their property.''

"She needs someone who cares about her, Val," he said patiently. "Really *cares*. Like Wyn."

"And Wyn never said a word." The devious old bitch!

He eyed her for a moment. "It slipped her mind, I guess." No word of criticism of his precious Wyn.

Valerie was deeply disturbed. "And she agreed?"

"Alex?" Alex was his private agony. He didn't intend to discuss her with Valerie.

"That's who all these questions are about, Scott," Valerie said. "I don't want her back in our lives. She's trouble."

"I happen to think so, too." He gave her an edgy look. "But it looks like it's going to happen."

"Then we'll just have to make the most if it." She feigned a warm smile of acceptance though the effort nearly choked her. "*You're* the one I'm really worried about. If there's any chance she can't resume her career, she'll turn back to you like a shot."

He looked up, beckoned the hovering waiter. "I don't think so, Val. I'm sure Alex knows she's three years too late."

"And there's *me*," she said, desperate to command his attention. Where *was* he?

"There is indeed."

The aquamarine eyes touched lightly on her face and breast, giving Valerie a tremendous erotic charge. If dear little Alex thought she was going to come between her and Scott, she had another think coming. Scott McLaren had *everything* she wanted in a man. Just to have him near her was to bask in the sun forever.

Valerie began to rack her brains for a plan. She wasn't sure how she was going to do it but she had to stop Alexandra Ashton from getting back on Main Royal.

*   *   *

He arrived at the hospital early enough to be able to
have a brief word with Alex's surgeon, who had already
established Scott McLaren was the nearest thing she had
to family. It was just as Alex had said. The prognosis
wasn't certain with respect to a resumption of her career.
Abnormal demands were placed on the bodies of dancers
and athletes. Alex's knee would have to withstand intense pressure. It was very much a wait-and-see, though
for normal purposes Mr Tomlinson expected the operation would be a complete success.

She was in the theatre longer than he'd been led to
expect, causing him an involuntary rush of anxiety. He
hadn't spent a single day in hospital in his whole life.
He'd even been born on Main Royal. Hospitals weren't
places he much liked. So much suffering. So many who
came out healed, ready to resume life. So many who
never made it. The anaesthesia was the worrying part.
Anaesthetists were clever people. A crucial part of the
team. A cousin, a thoracic surgeon, often referred to
himself as a plumber.

Alex wasn't all that long in the recovery room before
she came out of the anaesthetic, looking extraordinarily
like the ten-year-old he remembered.

"Scott!" She knew him instantly. Her small face, col-
ourless and framed by the hospital cap, twisted his heart.

"Just a few minutes, Mr McLaren," Sister advised.

"Thank you," he responded, just so grateful to *be*
there. He turned back to Alex and bent his head over
her. "You're going to be fine. I've already had a word
with Tomlinson. He's very pleased with how things
went."

Even then her eyelids were drooping, the thick dark
lashes sweeping her cheeks. "When will I see you?"
she managed in a whispery voice when he was almost
at the door.

"*Soon*, Alex," he promised. "I'll come for you when you're ready to leave."

That wasn't to happen. Two days before Alex was due to be discharged with Scott back on Main Royal, Alex had an unexpected visitor. As she lay in bed trying to interest herself in a new paperback, her leg feeling as if it was encased in iron, a tall, sophisticated blonde in a chic chrome yellow suit swept through the door carrying a sheaf of longstemmed pink roses. Two dozen at least, the clear cellophane wrapping tied with an extravagant silver-and-pink bow.

"Alex, remember me?" The visitor smiled brightly, hazel eyes conducting an intensive survey. "Valerie Freeman. I'm Scott's friend." Tone and expression were near confrontational.

Immediately Alex put down her book, doing her best to return the prescribed smile though she was intuitively aware this wasn't a *friendly* visit, more a testing of the waters. The odd thing was she felt Valerie Freeman *hated* her. But that was too absurd. She didn't even know her. "Of course I remember you, Valerie," she said. "How kind of you to visit me. And flowers! They're absolutely beautiful."

They were, the clear pink blooms just unfurling, the leaves lavish.

"I knew you'd like them," Valerie said carelessly, laying the sheaf down on the top of a cabinet. "Rather like carrying coals to Newcastle, though." She glanced briefly at the other massed arrangements. "But then you'd expect someone like you to have admirers."

There was something quite odd about the way she said it. "How did you know I was here?" Alex asked, weathering the studied appraisal. "Please do sit down. I'll call for someone to put the roses in water. The staff have been very good to me.''

''I'm not surprised.'' Valerie gave a short laugh. ''You look like you should be in one of the *children's* wards.'' In reality she was shocked and angered by the other young woman's beauty. Without make-up, her long hair scraped back except for a couple of sexy, cascading curls, her leg encased in plaster, Alexandra Ashton looked exquisite. A porcelain figurine. It was easy to see how she tugged at the heartstrings.

Valerie was sending out so many signals Alex felt bombarded. It was with relief she greeted the pretty freckle-faced nurse when she sailed into the room. ''Don't tell me, Alex,'' the nurse said cheerfully. ''*More* flowers. I can't bear it the way you're so popular. No one sends *me* flowers.''

''You wouldn't want your leg in plaster, either, would you?'' Alex teased. This particular nurse had been with her from the beginning.

The woman suddenly sobered. ''You're going to heal, Alex, never fear. You'll work your magic on stage again.'' She picked up the roses and slipped out of the room.

''I'll second that.'' Valerie settled herself in one of the armchairs, crossed her racehorse legs and looked down at them admiringly. She had chosen pale stockings that gave off an iridescent sheen. ''I've had the pleasure of seeing you many times. Not with Scott, I'm sorry to say. He positively loathes the ballet. Main Royal is *his* world.''

''I wouldn't say he loathed it,'' Alex corrected her because she felt she had to. ''More like cursed it.''

''You mean because it broke you two up?'' Valerie's tone stopped just short of aggression.

''That was quite a while ago,'' Alex parried.

"True."

"You didn't say how you knew I was here."

"Why, Scott told me, of course." Valerie frowned as though the very question was strange. "There's very little if anything he doesn't tell me. I had dinner with him only the other evening. That would have been the day you were admitted. I've been staying with my aunt and uncle for a couple of weeks. Naturally Scott promised to join me if he had a chance. As it happened, his visit worked out quite well for you, didn't it?"

"One always needs a friend, a familiar face," Alex said quietly, her heart heavy with this new knowledge. "And what are you doing with yourself these days, Valerie?"

"Oh, I haven't got a job, as such," Valerie said with no hint of defensiveness. "I'm not a dedicated little career woman like you. I help out on the property. Dad likes me around. He makes more than enough money for all of us. It's a full-time job leading the good life and of course there's Scott."

"Yes?" Alex lifted her winged brows. Let *her* say it.

Valerie gave a short, hard laugh. "You keep in touch with Wyn, don't you? You must know Scott and I are seriously involved."

It made painful listening. "I haven't kept up as much as I used to," Alex said evasively. "Scott is every woman's dream. I wish you luck."

"That's real nice of you, Alex," Valerie drawled, but it was easy to get a reading. "I appreciate that. It can't have been easy giving Scott up. Even for a brilliant career."

"No." She had to force herself to speak calmly.

"Of course the connection would have been broken long ago only for Wyn," Valerie insisted.

"Very likely. Scott isn't a particularly forgiving person."

"Oh, I know!" Valerie lifted her shoulders expressively. "He told me how Wyn wanted you to recuperate on the station. We both know he loves Wyn. He always wants to make her happy but he was pretty much *horrified* at the idea. I know I'm not letting the cat out of the bag when I say you're not one of his favourite people. You may not have broken his heart as I can attest but you certainly put a dent in his pride. Scott's as proud as a man gets and he's not used to rejection."

"Rejection's the wrong word." Alex was starting to feel utterly drained by her visitor. "Actually I haven't decided on anything," she said valiantly when she was cut to the heart.

Valerie nodded in sympathy. "I know exactly how you feel. *I* wouldn't want to go under those circumstances, either. It would be just too humiliating. It's not as though you don't have friends to turn to."

Alex had received all the messages loud and clear. Not that she didn't understand them. No sane woman would want to put temptation in her man's way. And that's how Valerie saw Scott; she had staked her claim. She had introduced herself as Scott's friend, from the bright, challenging look in her eyes, "friend" being a euphemism for lover. They *were* seriously involved; even Wyn had told her that. Valerie was right. Scott's love for his aunt had forced him to invite her to Main Royal. It was hardly the kind of invitation she needed or could now accept.

Valerie stayed for another ten minutes being desperately friendly. Her conversation was heavily sprinkled with references to the things she and Scott enjoyed together, including taking a brief idyllic break on one of the small, exclusive Barrier Reef islands.

"You know how difficult it is to get Scott away from Main Royal," she said, laughing. "It's almost an obsession. Thankfully I understand. I was born and bred on the land, as you know. Scott won't be taking any risks with *me*. We're two of a kind." She laughed merrily, all the while keeping a sharp eye on Alex's reactions.

Alex was tempted to say she didn't see Valerie as Scott's soul mate at all. Valerie's whole purpose in life seemed to be to have a good time. Didn't she *know* Scott's wife would have to assume any number of responsibilities? She would be expected to take an active part in the affairs of a vast, far-flung community. Scott's wife wouldn't be free to flit all over the country, going from one social occasion to the other. No one knew better than Alex how Scott defined the role of mistress of Main Royal. Valerie was thinking only up to the wedding.

"Well, it's been lovely chatting," Valerie said finally, rising to her slim height and carefully pressing the crease from her short skirt. "When you've fully recovered and I'm in town, we must have lunch sometime."

Alex doubted it.

"No need to mention my visit to Scott," she said, continuing to sound like Alex's fellow conspirator. "That's if you *see* him. We women need our private chats."

We do indeed, Alex thought. If only to clear the air. "I can understand you don't want me on Main Royal, Valerie, if that's what you mean." Alex faced the issue squarely.

The faintest flush appeared on Valerie's prominent cheekbones. "Come on, you can't blame me. You're very beautiful in your way. I can well understand how men fall in love with you. The thing is it's *Scott* you have to consider. Clearly he's given in to Edwina but he's deeply against your recuperating on Main Royal. I'm sorry, I do feel for you, but I'm not telling you anything you don't know.''

"No," Alex heard herself say in a philosophic tone. Pretend you don't care.

Valerie's relief and approval was palpable. "Well, I must fly," she said, half-turning her head to conceal her look of intense satisfaction. "I don't want to tire you. You're looking a bit peaky. Wyn will get over her disappointment, don't worry. She gets a bit lonely sometimes. She enjoys a woman's company. That's why I try to get over as often as possible. Take care now, Alex." She smiled. "My very best wishes for your speedy recovery."

"Thank you once again for my beautiful flowers," Alex said, thankful the intense scrutiny was finally over.

"Hey, I hope you get them back," Valerie joked. "That nurse took quite a fancy to them."

"I expect there's something more important to hand."

"How long will you be here?" Valerie paused at the door, her meticulously blunt-cut hair swinging around her shoulders.

"Another couple of days, my consultant, Mr Tomlinson, thinks."

"You'll have to get on to Edwina with your decision," Valerie urged. "I expect she'll be waiting. Let her down lightly, won't you? She really is fond of you."

"I know."

But it all had to do with Scott. And Scott didn't want her. That counted above all else. Just when she had been beginning to *dream* again, Valerie had wrenched her back to harsh reality.

There was nothing deader than a dead love. It's over, she thought. And *I* did it. It was like being tugged apart.

* * *

Wyn was filled with dismay when Alex rang to explain that grateful as she was for the offer to recuperate on Main Royal, she felt she should remain in her own apartment close to medical help and her friends who had arranged a support system.

It wasn't true. Her closest friends were still on tour, though there were one or two others she knew she could call on for help. While Wyn tried unsuccessfully to change her mind, assuring Alex they could provide her with all the attention she might need, Alex remained gently adamant.

"It can't be Scotty, surely, Alex?" Wyn forced herself to say it. "I don't know what impression you formed, but he is really very concerned about you. One can't kill all feeling, Alex."

She had denied all her own misgivings, not mentioning the fact Valerie had visited her. What was the point of stirring up trouble? Valerie wouldn't thank her. Neither would Scott. Wyn would only be deeply troubled. She had made Alex well aware she didn't consider Valerie *right* for her beloved nephew.

It was an upsetting phone call—Alex felt as if she wanted to cry—and when she rang off, pain was cutting at her nerves like a knife. She had hated disappointing the older woman when it sounded as though Wyn had really set her heart on her coming. Her feeling of letting her godmother down was enormous, but Alex told herself that in the end, none of them would be able to tolerate the strains. She had created another life. Even if things didn't go well for her and she couldn't return to the ballet, Scott had effectively distanced himself from her. He could pick and choose between a dozen eligible young women, Valerie of the long, beautiful legs among them. It was Wyn alone who was persisting with an old dream. Alex knew she could never expect the limitless love and comfort of the old days.

When McLaren returned to the house a little after dusk, his aunt was still sitting in her study with only one lamp on.

"Not still working, Wyn? You'll strain your eyes." He reached back to turn on the overhead light.

Wyn shook herself alert. "So did you finally catch The Ghost?"

"I'm almost too damned tired to talk." He flashed Wyn a white, wry smile, rubbing his brow where a lock of hair had tumbled. "He's in the holding yards at the Five Mile. Abe thinks we're wasting our time trying to make something of him, but I kinda like him. He's full of fire. All that *power!*"

Wyn gave him a nod of understanding. In her younger days she could ride with the best of them, compete in gruelling three-day events. "Alex put through a call to the house this afternoon," Wyn said, not looking him in the eye but straightening a folder on her desk.

"So when's she being discharged?" He turned, about to head for the shower. After a long, hard day in the saddle, it was something to look forward to.

Wyn looked at him standing there—darkly, rakishly handsome, raven hair tousled, a faint stubble of beard, red bandanna still tied carelessly around his neck, aqua eyes glittering like precious stones. He made the air reverberate. My *Scott*, she thought. My God, how I love him! He might as well be my son.

"Alex isn't coming." She tried to control her tone but it was full of a disappointment bordering on grief.

He took two steps back into the room, a dynamic, power-packed man, iron hard when he had to be, seeming to take forever before he exploded, "You mean she thought she would let it go until *now* to let you know? She must be due out.''

"Friday," Wyn confirmed, still thinking it awfully strange.

"Which is two days away, and I'm supposed to *fly* there?"

"She's not coming," Wyn repeated, swallowing the dryness in her throat. "She feels she should be near the hospital. Near her friends."

His eyes flashed blue fire. "When I looked in on her the morning after the operation, she damned well gave me to understand it was pretty well settled."

"So you said." Wyn was watching him carefully. Behind the explosive anger, she knew he was as upset as she was.

"So what changed her mind? Maybe the guy she's been linked with is back in the picture," he said disgustedly.

"I don't honestly know, Scott," Wyn said.

"Damn her," he muttered, then said it again, more harshly this time. "Alex sending us around in circles again. I did it for *you*, Wyn." Yet he saw Alex's pale face, her amber gaze in his mind's eye. God! She was in his blood.

"She would have been aware of it, dear," Wyn pointed out gently.

"So you put the blame squarely on *me*?"

Wyn shook her head, distressed. "How could you even say it? You're the best of men. Maybe I don't know Alex any more."

"Maybe we *never* knew her," McLaren said in a hard voice, his powerful lean body giving off heat. "We've offered, Wyn, and Alex has made her choice. Let it go."

"Strangely enough, it didn't sound much like she was enjoying it," Wyn reflected.

"That's just Alex wanting to be in your good books. Put the whole thing out of your mind, Wyn. You could knock yourself out trying to fathom what makes Alex tick."

With that, he stalked off. Hadn't he sworn he'd never be at Alex's mercy again? Why the hell didn't he stick to it?

CHAPTER FOUR

By THE end of the second week out of hospital, Alex was feeling desperately low in spirits. For someone who had spent every day of her life in rigorous training, she was well and truly earthbound. It wasn't easy for a creature used to floating free of gravity. What had one critic called her? An angel of lightness, movement and grace. He ought to see her now. She wasn't managing her crutches half as well as she had imagined. The thing was that she was skin and bone. No padding at all. Often she tried to lose herself in sleep the hours dragged so badly, but even in sleep, memories and emotions collided.

Perhaps in another month the plaster would be taken off and she could move around freely. But what of her knee? What of the severely torn ligaments? How well would they heal? Would the old injury affect her even in normal life? Occasionally the tears spurted but she wiped them away ruthlessly. She knew all about suffering. She had seen so much of it in hospital it seemed an absurdity to dwell on her own. There were worse things than having to let go of a brilliant career. She would have given up all thoughts of a career to have had her parents. In retrospect, she would never have left Scott for all the accolades she had won. When she wasn't actually *dancing*, there was a great emptiness inside her.

Scott.

Now more than ever, it was impossible to keep her thoughts of him at bay. No matter how much she had tried, and she *had*, she couldn't erase him from her heart and mind. He had staked an irrevocable claim on her very early in life. She hadn't heard from him once, not that she had expected to, but she and Wyn were in frequent touch. The last time they had spoken, Wyn had caught her at a bad moment when the huskiness from a little crying spell was still in her voice. She'd told Wyn she thought she was coming down with a cold. Wyn had said the necessary things. "Are you taking plenty of vitamin C?" But she knew Wyn hadn't been fooled.

It was when she was pouring herself a cup of coffee in her small kitchen that Alex heard the doorbell ring. It would probably be Brenda from next door to see if she wanted any groceries. Brenda, a recent divorcee in her mid-thirties, was very kind but she was suffering, too. It was there in her face and in her eyes and in the bitterness of her voice when she spoke of her ex-husband. Not that she overdid it, but Alex was feeling so vulnerable herself. Brenda's pain disturbed her.

She got her crutches into position and started the slow trek to the front door, calling, "Coming," as she struggled on her way. She was definitely getting better with the darn things, but they *hurt*. She even gave an exclamation of frustration and pain as she opened the main door, looking through the security door to where not petite Brenda was standing but a tall, powerfully built man casually dressed in a collarless white shirt and close-fitting jeans that hugged his lean, hard-muscled body.

"Scott!" Her heart gave a tremendous jolt.

"Your eyesight's good." His tone was sardonic. "Can I come in?"

"Of course." In her surprise and haste she stumbled, all but falling against the doorjamb.

"For God's sake!" His hands flew out as if he wanted to seize the security door and pull it off its hinges. "Take it easy, Alex. Stand still for a moment and balance yourself.''

"*Me*, balance myself?" It struck her as funny. Alexandra Ashton, whose balances opened like flowers.

"Stop it." He spoke sharply, deliberately quelling the outburst of discordant laughter.

Even to Alex, it sounded a little manic. The awful truth of it was that she felt like she was about to go to pieces. *Scott* on her doorstep. What had he come for? To demand she return with him? To tell her Wyn was afraid for her?

Lord, she was afraid for herself.

She unlocked the security door and he opened it out, stepping over the threshold and towering over her.

"Look at you."

"Don't tell me. I'm not looking my best," she said with a wry smile.

He turned directly to face her, his scrutiny keen. She was all eyes, sooty shadows beneath. Fragile as eggshell china. Her beautiful hair was caught back from her face, piled high at the crown, the bulk of it tumbling down her back. She was wearing a loose, creamy summer dress sprigged with roses that skimmed her body and fell almost to her ankles so the plaster cast wasn't much in evidence. He could feel his hard-won detachment beginning a long slide but he hauled it back. He could do it. He'd had a lot of practice.

"Well?" Her mouth was curved up slightly as she waited for his judgment.

He gave a short laugh. "Don't go fishing, Alex. You look great. Too skinny, of course." He willed himself to look away from the enchanting face, the swan's neck, the outline of her breasts. Small but exquisite, their nipples peaked against the soft, lightweight material. Clearly she wasn't wearing a bra, but then it would be difficult for her to get in and out of clothes. Angry with himself, he moved. It was safer. Much safer. Any contact with Alex was electric. Then his innate gallantry seized him. "Here, let me help you." He turned back. "It must be hell for a dancer to be immobilised."

"You can say that again! But I'm getting there." She forced herself to move off with as much confidence as she could muster, a high level of exhilaration mixed up with a strange wariness.

To make it worse, she *wanted* him to take hold of her. To lift her, to crush her. She wanted to feed off his blazing aura, his abundant strength. You make me strong, Scott. You make me free.

She made it to an armchair, easing herself into it, while he took charge of her crutches, placing them neatly beside her. "I was having a cup of coffee when you arrived. I expect it's cold now, but there's more in the percolator. Would you like some?"

"Why not?" he answered brusquely. It would give him a few moments to get himself together. Damn Alex. She made him *hurt*, she was so far under his skin.

Waiting quietly, Alex felt her emotions escalating. At least Scott had smiled at her though there was a sharp contrast between the white smile and the glittering eyes. Maybe in his way he was as trapped as she was. Trapped in the past.

"Have you eaten?" he demanded, coming back into the living room.

"I'm fine." She waved a nonchalant hand. "I had a sandwich around two. What about you? Make yourself one. There's fresh bread, ham, some chicken in the fridge."

"So someone *does* help you?"

"I have friends, Scott. I'm not *alone*," she said firmly.

"Like hell you aren't." He dismissed her lie with a shake of his head.

"There's Brenda next door," she called after him, but he didn't respond.

A few minutes later he came back with two cups on a tray, setting it down on the low coffee table. "No sugar?" he asked in an acerbic voice.

"I'm used to it."

"You used to have quite a sweet tooth as a child."

A freeze frame in his mind. The young Alex in her school uniform happily downing the bar of chocolate he had bought her. Even in her school uniform she'd been an incredibly sexy little thing. Exotic yet innocent. She'd put quite a few of his girlfriends' noses out of joint.

The sweetest smile graced her lips. "I still remember all those bars of chocolate you used to bring me at school. We were *starved* for sweets."

It was easy for her to pick up on his thoughts. A muscle in his jaw jumped. "Wyn wanted me to call in on you. Check on your progress."

"Surely you didn't come all this way for that?" She was shocked.

"Not at all." He couldn't help the curtness of his tone. "I'm attending a dinner for the Premier tonight. A few of us have been asked to speak."

"Why didn't you refuse? You can't like him?" she half joked.

"I don't have to like him. I'm prepared to give him time to prove himself."

Alex shrugged. "I'm sure you'll be very well received. Apart from what you *say*, your voice compels people to listen. Quite an asset."

"In this case I hope so," he said dryly. "I'll be saying a few words about the plight of the man on the land."

"With the power and influence of the McLaren chain behind you."

"There's that." He picked up the coffee and handed it to her, then moved himself away to the sofa on the other side of the table.

Alex got the message. He wanted to be as far away from her as possible.

"Wyn is still hoping you'll spend some time with her," he said, frowning slightly. "Something about your last phone call upset her."

"Wyn's love and generosity bring me to tears," she admitted.

He shoved back against the sofa so abruptly she felt a momentary flutter of alarm. "You have shadows under your eyes and your hands are shaking."

She looked down at them, buried them in the soft folds of her dress. "I know. I have to tell you, Scott, when you want to be, you're quite scary."

"Rubbish," he rasped. "More like you can't twist me around your little finger like you used to." She most likely *could* if she tried, he thought with black humour.

"It's not what I'm trying to do," she protested. "It's not easy being like this."

"I *know* it isn't. In fact, it must be damned difficult being on your own. Don't try to tell me about these friends of yours. There may be a woman in the next apartment, thank God, but all your closest friends are still touring. They *can't* help you when you most need it."

Alex was forced to let the charge hang in the air. It was perfectly true. "Another month," she said finally. "It will pass."

"It could work out to be longer." He gave her an assessing look. "Maybe eight weeks in all. You told me that yourself."

She regarded him gravely, perched on the fine line between pleasure and sadness. "I'm a quick healer, Scott. I always have been. Remember when I—"

"Alex, I don't hold on to my memories," he said crisply.

She laughed even though she was giving herself away. "I go over mine all the time."

"I hope they've got nothing to do with *me*."

"You're so bitter, Scott," she said in a hushed voice.

"So far as you're concerned. Yes." He heaved a weary sigh.

"Is that why you're sitting on the opposite side of the table?"

"Just a little protection, Alex," he mocked. "I'm mortal man. You dabble in magic." A little pause. "Drink up your coffee," he suggested. "It doesn't take long to go cold."

"I don't really need it," she confessed. "I was just filling in time." She started to lean forward but the table was too far away.

"Here, let me help you." He stood up, moving around to her with his lithe big-cat tread. He was literally breathtaking. It was a feat to conceal her reactions. Nevertheless she found herself edging back into the corner of the sofa as he approached. She had this strange feeling of déjà vu. It swept over her in a wave. "Alex, what's the matter?" he asked sharply, taking the coffee cup from her and setting it down on the table with a thud.

"I..." She shook her head, uncertain how to respond. Maybe she was going to snap at long last.

"It's okay to tell me," he urged, unnerved by the abrupt change in her demeanour. "Alex? What the hell!" He sat down on the sofa beside her, half-turning her to him with one hand on her shoulder.

"I suppose it has to do with Valerie?" she asked raggedly, caught by surprise.

"In part." His voice was dark, the aquamarine eyes not smiling. "I hate being manipulated by you, Alex. You're not going to get the chance to screw up my life again. No mad passion. No betrayal."

"Just Valerie."

His expression hardened as he met her shimmering gaze. "What *is* it you're trying to get me to do, Alex?" There was a decided edge to his voice.

Only then did she realise her whole body was flowing towards him. "Nothing. I'm so sorry, Scott." She tried to pull back, only his hand tightened.

"What is it they say? Face the demons. Make them go away."

"Not like *this*." She read the expression in his eyes, was disturbed by it.

"It's only a kiss, Alex. Why should you be the one to panic?"

She felt the blush all over her body. "Because you're using your power *against* me."

"So it's finally dawned on you." His extraordinary eyes gleamed. "That's it exactly. I'm *challenging* you. Maybe expending one's pain is part of the healing process."

His hand moved very gently from her cheek to her shoulder, skimmed her breast, his fingers seductively teasing the already taut nipple that swelled to his touch. The same subtle perfume hung over her. The sweet aroma that was her own skin. Desire was an invincible force, he thought, and nothing to be done about it. It left one mindless of everything. Except *one* thing.

Their eyes held for a single heartbeat, the expression in his leaving Alex in no doubt that this was a kind of revenge. Three years on. She *knew* it, yet the ache inside

There was no escape. She couldn't leap up
away.

"Tell me right now," he said flatly. "Are you
You don't look like you've been eating properly. Ther
not a lot of security around here, either. Has that bee
worrying you?"

She just shook her head, sitting quite still. How could
she tell him she was *grieving*? On so many fronts. Not
the least of them losing him. She wanted to ask him
about Valerie Freeman but Scott would never share anything with her again.

"All right, so you don't want to talk about it." His
detachment was slipping but there didn't seem anything
he could do about it. "Is it some man?"

Only *you*, she thought. That didn't make her feel better.

"The guy who's supposed to look like Baryshnikov?
You miss him?"

She had to laugh. It was so absurd. "Scott, Victor's
gay."

He shrugged. "So where does that leave us?"

"The fact is I'm just a bit low." Her tone was full of
a kind of melancholy, much as she tried to conceal it.

"Maybe being on your own wasn't such a good
idea," he pointed out. "You always did suffer from th
sin of pride."

"Really? I thought it was the other way around."

"Of course it is." He laughed ironically. For a m
ment he forgot himself, reaching out and tucking b
a long, spiralling curl from her face.

"You don't want me on Main Royal," she said s
ly. "There's no use denying it."

"You're absolutely right, Alex." He cupped her
brought her mouth to him. A bare two inches aw

her was overwhelming, taking charge of her physical being. She tried to remind herself he wasn't *her* Scott any longer, but her body was dissolving...bathed in the most exquisite heat. He was turning her to flame.

"Let's drown together, Alex," he said a little brutally. "Remember the pool of forgetfulness?"

The descent of his mouth was slow, so tantalisingly slow it was a torment. He was making her supremely aware he was the one in control. And he was *enjoying* it. Even armed with that knowledge, Alex gave herself hopelessly away. It had been so long. An eternity since she had known the incomparable excitement of a man's sexual drive. Or more specifically, Scott's. After Scott, she had been unable to connect with anyone. Scott was quite singular.

Her mouth flowered at the first contact, her tongue eager to mate with his. This was one of her weak moments when she was forced to shed her mask. The old magic had taken hold. The same burning desire, sweet, fierce, primal. She wanted to communicate her hopes, her fears, her secret dreams. The very slowness of his ministrations only heightened the excitement, though she wasn't that far gone she couldn't recognise the rapture was shot through with a certain anguish. Self-humiliation perhaps? This was her Scott. Then again, he *wasn't*. Either way, everything revolved around him. Her. Her life.

What was he trying to teach her?

A lesson?

He was too good at it.

Perfect.

Her wonderful Scott was after revenge. True. True. *True*. How could he be such a monster? she thought wildly, concentrating now with all her might on calming her aroused and trembling body.

"Don't." Her voice was stricken, yet powerfully excited.

"Your idea, Alex," he drawled, his tone deep, dark, intimate, but totally without the tenderness she had never been able to forget. He drew her even closer, savouring the scent of her, the achingly delicate fragility of her never-to-be-forgotten body. Alex, the grounded butterfly, one brilliant wing clipped. "Neither of us is exactly a virgin," he taunted her.

Oh, that was *wicked*, that reminder. It kindled her quick temper. She stiffened, angling away as anger bubbled to the surface, overriding her molten torpor. She couldn't understand why she had allowed him to trap her. "Let me go, Scott." She pushed fiercely against his chest. She might just as well have been pushing against a brick wall.

"Maybe for the time being," he mocked, making an elaborate play of removing his hands from her small, swelling breasts. "There's Valerie, sure. But I have to hand it to you, Alex. There's only *one you*."

She lifted a shaking hand, tossed back her glowing hair. "Are you sure you should have handed me that vital piece of information?"

"Hell, Alex, I don't have much choice," he jeered.

"So you haven't buried all the pain, have you? Or the hurt?"

"Well now, I thought I had." With indolent grace he folded his hands behind his head. "Put it down to a kind of experiment. I had to find out. Maybe I'm stuck with it. Who knows?"

Little flames danced in her gold-flecked eyes. "It's not the way *I* want it," she said. He wasn't going to quiet her.

"Really?" He gave a maddening laugh. "Is that supposed to make me like you any better?"

She could feel the endless turmoil that churned inside both of them; the tension strung tight like piano wire.

"You and Wyn are the only family I have left in this world," she tried to explain, her voice brittle with the effort to control it.

His expression was full of mistrust, deeply cynical. "Alex, that's *nauseating*."

My God, what's happened to us? she thought. We were absolutely everything to each other. Now this. She bit hard on her underlip, crimson like crushed rose petals, pulsing from the deep, hard pressure of his mouth. "Think what you like," she said fiercely. "It still doesn't change the fact it's the truth."

"Is it?" He bent forward suddenly, causing her to arch back as in some crazy tango. "You show Wyn how much you love her by staying *away*? Is that it? You allow her to think you're coming, then you cry off two days before you're due out of hospital?" His blue-green eyes glittered. "What the hell were you thinking? I'd really like to know." He took hold of her wrist, circling it with thumb and finger.

Couldn't he feel her pulse racing, the fever in her blood? "I know how you feel about my coming back to Main Royal, Scott," she said emotionally. "You're only doing it for Wyn. I had to make a decision. I have my pride. I acted on those feelings. *Your* feelings. If it were only *Wyn*—"

"Go on." He flung her hand off. "You want *me* out?"

"Yes." It came out hard and cold when she was lying. Couldn't he see it in her face?

Evidently he did. "Sorry, Alex, I can't wear that one. A moment ago I had you shaking in my arms."

She didn't answer. She couldn't. There was no way to hide it.

He looked at her bitterly as though stung by her beauty. "Whether you believe it or not, I want you to get better, Alex. I want your leg to mend. *Perfectly.* I want you to get back to your career."

"You who loathes the ballet?"

"What are you talking about?" He frowned. "Some of it is a dead bore, but I could watch you forever. You're a *dream.*" His expression was brooding and respectful all at the same time. "It was brutal of you not to tell me about your ambitions. How badly you wanted fame. Anyway—" he shrugged the past off "—I don't want to take you on any guilt trip. You're much too vulnerable for that. Wyn thinks you don't really want to be on your own. She's very insistent about that. You know what she's like when she gets the bit between her teeth. She wanted me to check on you."

"Dear Wyn," Alex said softly. "You'll have to tell her I'm finding it a bit of a grind."

"Alex, I won't be there much of the time," he said wearily. "The week after next I have the two-week trip to Japan lined up. You'll enjoy being back with Wyn and you won't be bothered by my presence."

She wanted to tell him about Valerie but couldn't. "I know I can count on you to tell me I've overstayed my welcome," she said with a glimmer of a smile.

"Does that mean you'll come back with me?"

"I'm not sure." She was deeply mindful of her changed position, of Valerie's visit. "Can you give me overnight to think about it?"

"No, I can't," he said flatly. "So don't go waffling on. You look like you haven't had one decent night's sleep, let alone a square meal."

"Do you mind!" She tilted her chin. "I'm very good at looking after myself."

His smile though sarcastic was a blazing illumination

in his bronzed face. "Try to appease me, Alex, for old times' sake."

"Have you discussed this with Valerie?" she felt constrained to ask.

"Are you crazy? Why would I have to get Val's permission?"

"Good grief, isn't she the woman in your life?" she countered. "Surely she's entitled to some consideration?"

He took his time to answer. No doubt counting to ten. "You let *me* worry about Valerie, Alex."

"Okay," she said, shrugging. "She must have some misgivings. Most people knew we were on the eve of getting engaged."

His handsome face lit with ironic laughter. "You mean you *remember*?"

Her ivory skin flushed. She'd asked for it.

"I guess Val appreciates our mad passion was just that. Ancient history. Not a problem."

"Then I'll come."

He stood up instantly. Dynamic. Unique. "Just so you don't change your mind, I'd like to leave this afternoon."

"What?" She stared up at him in consternation. "Scott, I need more time. I really do."

His smile grew taut. "Alex, you don't have to move. You can sit on the sofa. I'll grab your things and shove them into a suitcase. Time's getting away." He flicked a glance at his gold watch.

"You don't know what I want," she protested.

"Why don't we get you whole first?" he countered oddly.

"Scott, Scott, please." He was like a whirlwind, making her dizzy.

"Why don't I carry you into the bedroom?" he suggested with a kind of black humour. "You can direct operations. Between the two of us, we should be able to do your packing. You'll need next to nothing." She opened her mouth to speak but recognised the futility of it. He slipped an arm under her and gathered her up, his expression considering, even a little angry. "What the heck do you weigh? Even with a plaster cast on your leg, you're a featherweight."

Somehow she was able to joke when she could feel the heat of his body through the fine linen. "Have you ever seen a *fat* ballerina?"

"Miss Piggy?" His smile was silky smooth but strong emotion gyrated behind his eyes. With great care, he carried her into her bedroom, stooping low as she came against him on the bed. "Remember how I used to carry you into the sand-dunes? Remember what I used to do to you? There wasn't an inch of you I didn't kiss. No secret place. I knew you like I know myself."

There was no answer possible from Alex. She *burned*. Still tormented by the old passionate tyrannies and no way to assuage them.

His eyes looked into hers—beautiful, hostile. "For all you did to me, I still feel desire. Now isn't that too damned perverse?"

The emotions that were driving him were driving her. "Maybe desire doesn't go away," she heard herself murmuring.

"That's good for someone who can turn it on and off." His eyes narrowed. "You don't like letting go, do you, Alex?"

She saw how utterly convinced of it he was. Convinced and contemptuous.

She let out a shaky breath. "I don't know what you're getting at."

He seized on that. "Oh yes, you do, you little fraud. You were *everything* in my life."

An answering anger tore through her. "You might remember. *I loved you, too.*" She spoke so fiercely her voice shook.

"Did you? Did you *really*, Alex?" He leaned over her as she lay helpless, one hand moving to encircle her throat.

She could feel the soft violence. "Are you going to kill me for it?"

Urgent seconds throbbed by while they stared at each other, a kind of rage gathering.

"There was a time I could have throttled you," he muttered, abruptly straightening up. "You left me so bereft. But that time's gone, Alex. Gone, gone, *gone*. The Alex of my dreams was an exquisite mirage. You still have it in you to make me lose my head, but my heart will never be yours again."

CHAPTER FIVE

AT FIRST it looked like a speck in the hot cobalt sky, then a powerful white bird gliding on a down wind. Wyn stood on the veranda of the homestead, one hand shading her eyes as she watched the Beech Baron make its descent over the vast plains and ancient plateaus, the colourful rocks and jagged gorges, the endless maze of dark green billabongs and wind-rippled sands that made up Main Royal Station. There was a flame of joy inside her that not even the unwelcome presence of another could dim.

Alex, her little Alex, was coming home! Wyn loved her goddaughter so much the enforced distance between them had been very hard to bear. Why, she had been there at the very moment Alexandra Edwina Ashton had come into the world. She had held her darling little friend Maureen's hand, told Maureen with tears in her eyes that she had a "little princess in her own image". Tragic Maureen of the huge amber eyes and blazing chestnut hair. She had held the infant Alex, the prettiest baby she had ever seen, in her arms at the baptismal font, Alex strangely red-faced and squalling when she was such a serene, happy baby. She remembered the otherworldly look in Paul's grey eyes when he bent to kiss her.

"Bless you, Wyn. We have a great need of you."

Such a strange thing for him to say when he and Maureen had the whole world at their feet. Had father and daughter foreseen the future? Wyn had pondered that question over and over. The Ashtons, her tragic

74

young friends, destined never to grow old. Wyn kept them locked away safely inside her heart. They never left her. Her sacred duty to their child would remain with her until she died. Not that it had ever been a duty, but a source of great pride and happiness. Never once in all the years had she seen Alex indulge in a single mean or selfish act. Her character was warm, open, generous, loving.

Scott had never fully understood Alex's desire to spread her wings, to prove her worth as an individual. Scott had been the symbol of masculine power, the linchpin around which they all turned. He should have permitted Alex her dreams at least for a few years, but he had seen Alex's ambitions as a wilful act of defection, a rebellion against his love and authority. Clearly he had suffered lasting damage because of Stephanie's cruel treatment, which had made him all the more severe on Alex. Alex had too much spirit to view herself as secondary to any man, even Scott, her hero. Neither of them had truly understood what drove the other. In the end, both of them had lost out.

Scott for all his toughness *needed* Alex. It had become clear to Wyn through Alex's long letters that Alex's dream of becoming a leading dancer wasn't everything in the way of fulfilment, either. Both continued to be in conflict with life, and with one another. Scott didn't know what to do with all the strong emotions inside him. His relationship with Valerie Freeman, which had survived longer than the others, lacked the emotional intensity that was an integral part of Scott's nature. After the initial sick shock of Alex's injury, Wyn saw this time of convalescence as a second chance for the two young people she loved most in this world.

A clipped voice behind her recalled Wyn to the present.

"It won't be long now before they touch down."

Wyn turned back a moment, saw Valerie, reed slim in an expensive pink silk shirt and matching linen trousers, her trademark blunt-cut hair gleaming. She was lounging back gracefully in a white wicker armchair, but Wyn realised she was very tense inside. Intense, angry, aggressive.

"Scott *will* be surprised to see you, Valerie," she offered in her quiet-spoken way. Valerie had literally turned up on their doorstep less than an hour ago. Unannounced. Uninvited. A brilliant smile masking her strong antagonism.

"But thrilled, I should think," Valerie countered, bridling. "I just want to put my mind at rest about this, Edwina. I'm not happy with the situation. I'm worried Alex will want to resume the relationship. A woman like that always wants to see if she still has the same power over a man." Her voice hardened, became thick with resentment. "Lord knows she's well used to playing the enchantress on stage."

Wyn turned away so Valerie wouldn't see the anger in her eyes. "Alex is such a warm, expressive person, Valerie. She gives so much of herself onstage and off. I've missed her terribly."

Valerie gave a short laugh. "I'm sure you have, but we have to face this, Edwina. Hopefully together. Alex hurt and disappointed Scott dreadfully. He's over that now. We have a future together. I just don't want Alex to start up any power games to fill in the time. I've played second fiddle to her long enough. I'm the woman in Scott's life and I won't be passed over even for a few weeks. Your Alex might look like a piece of porcelain but she has incredible stamina. She'll put this injury behind her and go back to her own world. In the meantime I don't want her destroying mine."

Valerie was so forthright, laying her cards on the table, that Wyn thought she would add a timely warning of her own. "I don't think you've found the key to Scott yet, Valerie. If he loves you, you have nothing to fear, surely?"

"He *does* love me," Valerie was sufficiently far gone as to almost snap in the presence of Miss Edwina McLaren of Main Royal Station. "I know he was on the brink of making a real commitment before this news about Alex," she continued, her tone modified. "I realise you're very fond of her, Edwina, but please take a little time to think about me."

Wyn thought about her. Too often. "I realise your position, Valerie," she said gently, "but even when we want something very badly, that doesn't always mean we're going to get it. I don't want to see you hurt, either."

Valerie pounced on that. "You're not on *my* side, Edwina."

Wyn couldn't deny it. To her mind, something about Valerie Freeman cast a shadow. "My dear, if Scott loves you and wants to make you his wife, that's it as far as I'm concerned."

"You have a lot of influence with Scott, Edwina. You *know* you do," Valerie persisted.

"Certainly. We're very close." Wyn's voice remained calm and courteous.

"He would never have invited Alex back to Main Royal if it hadn't been for you." Valerie's tone was accusatory.

"I'm not so sure of that, Valerie, and I don't think you should be, either. Scott has looked out for Alex since she was a lost and lonely grief-stricken little girl. He has a deep protective streak. He many well have had concerns about Alex's coming back, but deep down he didn't want her to have to struggle on her own. There's not only the physical injury to Alex. There's also a brilliant career being put in jeopardy.''

"So you believe she'll go back to it if she can?" Valerie looked up, surprised by the remark.

"It took a lot of hard work and determination to get her where she is, let alone the severance from Scott. Both of them led with their hearts, not their heads. As far as I'm concerned, we'll have to take each day as it comes. Alex isn't a cruel young woman, Valerie. She won't be out to make trouble. She's well aware all our lives have changed.''

"I certainly hope so,'' Valerie said and pushed herself to her feet. "But you can't blame me for being anxious. Thank you so much for putting me up for a few days.''

Wyn decided to ignore that. She had never known a time when Valerie didn't invite herself.

Her heart thudding, Alex tried to control the feeling of homecoming that threatened to overwhelm her. Coming back to Main Royal was like being reborn. She gloried in the view of the station from the air. It was the best way to see it: vast, formidable, colourful, surreal. It had an other-world feel to it that had nothing in common with the lushness of the coastal strip that surrounded the continent.

This was the land of the invincible sun, of desert and drought, of infinite lines of spume-tossed red dunes that still resembled uncannily the inland sea of prehistory. From the air, one could appreciate the incredible topography, the criss-crossing of the countless water channels that gave the region its name and allowed the Channel Country to run its great herds. This was the real home of the cattle kings. The home they loved passionately.

Beneath the bold, sun-baked earth lay zillions of dormant flower seeds, the greatest accumulation of seeds on earth, that within a month of rain transformed the parched earth into the garden of Eden. The sight once seen could never be forgotten. It made one believe there was no death but endless rebirth. Not death but *survival*.

Scott had explained it all to her when she was a little girl, when it was most important to her that she not lose sight of her parents. They were there for her, he told her, *waiting*. Like the miracle of the wildflowers. From her first sight of them, she had never doubted it.

To the west beneath the cloudless blue sky lay the eroded breakaway plateau top called Kurakai. Kurakai was her favourite desert mesa on the whole of Main Royal. When she had first sighted it at the age of ten, she had named it Magic Mountain because it changed colour right through the day, from pale blue to pink, rose and bright red in the midday glare, then back through the spectrum until it turned mauve and finally a wonderful violet. Later she came to realise that all the rocks of the Interior changed colour, a desert phenomenon.

As a child she had cried with joy when the desert blazed into life, clapped her hands at the endless vistas of flowers when the plains and sandy deserts were heavily embroidered by a dense carpet of everlastings as far as the eye could see. The colours had never intermingled. They were quite separate, with vast tracts of papery white, then bright pink, then blazing yellow. Such a great diversity of wildflowers! But she had a special love for the cheerful little paper daisies that showed their cheeky faces to the sun.

Scott took his eyes briefly from the control panel to study her rapt profile. It had been a long, exhausting afternoon and not a particularly good flight; they had encountered a bad pocket of turbulence coming in over the desert, but never once had she murmured or offered a word of complaint. He knew he had pushed her, perhaps too hard since the trauma of her operation, hospitalisation and largely fending for herself had greatly increased her fragility, though he knew better than anyone that Alex was a superb athlete. She had studied gymnastics as well as ballet. In reality, the romantic creature that was Alexandra Ashton was extremely strong. Both physically and mentally. He had to keep remembering that. The heartbreaking little girl was long gone.

"How's it going?" he asked now.

She turned her face from the window to sigh blissfully. "It's wonderful to be back. Always in my mind Main Royal is a world apart."

"But it can't match the excitement of the stage?" he challenged, brooding almost.

"They're two entirely *different* worlds."

"One to give your allegiance to. One to leave?"

God help her, she had. "I wanted to *prove* myself, and I have. You're not the only one who can reach the top."

His eyes flashed. "Reach the top? What the heck does that mean? I *inherited* Main Royal. It will endure after I've passed on."

Alex slumped for the first time in deference to her aching spine. "You know what I mean. Running it is a very serious business. You wouldn't be chairman of McLaren Enterprises if you couldn't handle the job. The family look to you for your leadership and financial expertise, as well as support. You had to get yourself a degree in commercial law."

"And it's come in handy, but you're not telling me you thought we were in some sort of *competition*?"

"*I* was," she said. "I see that now. I knew I couldn't match you but I had a hunger to try."

Surprise and frustration warred in his eyes. "Why

didn't you ever tell me you wanted so much more? A career. You didn't even give me the opportunity to come to terms with it.''

She put her hand to her head. "Oh God, Scott, can't you *understand*?''

"I understand I'm no closer to figuring you out than I was then,'' he returned bluntly. "You told me you loved me. You wanted to marry me. Make Main Royal your home. Can you blame me for *believing* you?''

She flushed under his stare. "I *should* have told you I wanted a chance but I was afraid.''

He clearly rejected that. "Come off it, Alex. You're not afraid of anything. Anyone who dared to do the things you did can never describe themselves as timid.''

"As I recall, anything I dared to do met with your strong disapproval,'' she answered hotly.

"Alex, I was dedicated to saving your pretty little neck. Everyone on the station was. You were always trying to demonstrate your skills.''

"Skills *you* taught me.''

"Maybe. The truth is you were a natural. A natural athlete with a sweet, gentle way with horses. Shooting was the only thing you didn't really like, but you knew you were going to have to handle a gun. The wild bush isn't suburbia.''

"All those hours of practice!'' she murmured, looking back.

"All I know is that you learned how to handle yourself, and most importantly, to protect yourself.'' He said no more until they lined up with the all-weather runway, ready to land. "Wyn is thrilled out of her mind. For all we've lost, you'll always stay close to her heart.''

Wearing an ear-to-ear grin, Abe was there to greet them, his black, weathered face in stark contrast to his thick crop of snow-white curls. Flanking him, barking joyously, tails thumping, were Rory and Beau, the station cattle dogs, caught up in the welcome. Clearly they remembered Alex, responding ecstatically to the sound of her voice as she called to them.

"You'd better stop, Alex," Scott finally advised her. "They're getting too excited." He quietened them with a firm order, carrying Alex to the open jeep where Abe was holding the door as if she were royalty.

"It's a great joy to see you, Miss Alex," he said, benediction in his voice. Abe bore himself like the revered tribal elder he was. "We were so sorry to hear about your accident, but we're gonna make you better. You're so powerful *skinny*." He couldn't keep the concern out of his voice.

"A porcelain doll," Scott added briefly.

"I'm so glad you're here to greet me, Abe." Alex smiled back at her old friend and mentor. "I feel better already. You've always been my friend."

"Don't you mean greatest slave, Princess?" Abe chuckled, using his old childhood nickname for her. "I seem to remember trailin' you around so you wouldn't land yourself in all sorts of trouble." He smiled that wide grin again.

"And we're mightily in your debt, Abe," Scott said, looking down at Alex. The brilliant light washed her bright hair and flawless skin.

"She does look tired, though," Abe said, concern clouding his broad face. "All big eyes and dark circles, but as I say we're gonna look after her."

Alex looked at him with affection. "It's lovely to see you, Abe. I truly, truly mean it."

"I know you do, Princess." Abe's liquid black eyes glistened. "When you're rested we can have a long talk. I want to learn what I can do to help that injured leg along."

Alex looked down at the bulky shape. "It's going to *need* your magic, Abe."

"And the damn fool really dropped you?" Abe asked in disgust and amazement.

"He didn't *drop* me, Abe. He didn't *catch* me. I was flying like a bird."

Abe shook his head and made a hissing sound through his teeth before turning away. "Want me to drive you up to the house, Boss?"

"It's all right, Abe," Scott answered casually. "You could meet me at the Oonta yards in about an hour. Bring Mick with you."

"Right." Abe tipped his battered akubra. "I'll see you later, Miss Alex."

"You bet!" Alex gave a smile that showed her warm heart.

"By the way, Boss…" Abe beckoned to Scott as though he wanted to speak to him privately.

"It can keep, Abe." Scott moved to get into the jeep.

"Miss Freeman is up at the homestead," Abe offered out of the corner of his mouth. "Arrived in her dad's helicopter more than an hour ago."

Scott's expression registered nothing. "Thanks, Abe."

Alex too kept silent although she couldn't control a clutch of dismay. She had so wanted her homecoming, if that was what it was, to be private. Family. She hadn't reckoned on Valerie. Neither had Scott, apparently, if Abe thought he had to warn him.

Warn him? What a curious thought. If Scott was in love with Valerie, wouldn't he want to see her as much as possible? He had certainly been obsessive enough about her. In fact, he hadn't wanted Alex out of his sight.

"Won't be long now," Scott told her briefly, aware of her pallor and the fine beading of perspiration that dampened the stray curls at her temples. At least he'd got her here, but at a cost.

"I can't wait to see Wyn." Alex took a deep breath of fresh air, pure, dry, spiced with aromatic bush scents. No city pollution here.

"Val must have wanted to be on hand to add to the welcome," he said smoothly, probably tongue-in-cheek.

"More likely she's aching to see you." Didn't she know all about that kind of ache herself? Waking up in the middle of the night, her mind filled with memories of Scott, her body yearning for his never-to-be-forgotten touch.

"I guess," he said, shrugging. "It means an overnight stay. Usually does."

"She's very attractive."

"Without question." He glanced at her sharply and smiled. A tigerish sort of smile.

"I'll always wish you health and happiness, Scott."

"Well, thanks, Alex. Too bad you didn't go the right way about it."

Something of the old rebellion flared in her. "You didn't exactly acquit yourself wonderfully well, either."

His reaction was instant. "Hell, Alex, I would have given you anything...*everything*."

"Except...*time*."

"You're dead right," he said briefly. "I wanted you. I needed you. You wanted something else."

She was bested and knew it.

At the homestead, Wyn and Valerie were standing side by side on the veranda, but when the jeep entered the circular drive, Wyn took off down the short flight of steps with a sprightliness of a woman half her age. "Alex, darling," she cried, arms flung out, her voice full of joyous welcome.

Alex, darling. Up on the veranda, Valerie savagely

mimicked Wyn's tone beneath her breath. Hot rage flooded her. The scheming little bitch was back to make trouble. She knew it with a great certainty. Nothing good could possibly come of this visit. *Alex, darling* had a powerful ally in Edwina. They were the same kind of people.

The jeep had barely come to a standstill before the two women were locked in an embrace, Wyn bending into the open jeep, Alex with her arms flung around her godmother's neck.

Beautiful! Valerie thought. It would really make you cry, only she was light-years away from crying. She was hopping mad.

"Wyn." Alex was a little girl again, desperate for comfort. "It's been so *long*."

"I'd begun to think I'd never see you again," Wyn answered in a muffled, emotional voice. "You're so *thin*!" For a moment, concern clouded her radiant face.

"Heavens. You're all telling me that! Don't worry about it," Alex exclaimed. "Home cooking will soon fatten me up."

"Let's get her out of the jeep," Scott said a little curtly, his heart twisting at their emotional meeting.

"Of course, darling." Wyn moved aside quickly. "We'll get you up to the house and make you comfortable, Alex. It must have been a long trip."

"I want to see the sunset from the veranda." Alex circled her arm lightly around Scott's neck, revelling in his strength and nearness. "No matter how beautiful sunset is in the city, it doesn't compare with our desert sunsets."

"Of course not," Wyn agreed happily, at long last remembering Valerie. She spoke in an undertone. "Valerie is here, dear. You know, Valerie Freeman."

"Don't be silly, Wyn. Of course she knows her." Scott glanced at his aunt.

"Yes, of course. I..." For a minute, off guard, Alex almost blurted out that Valerie had visited her in hospital. "It's a big surprise." She turned her head back towards Wyn and gave her a little wink.

"Cut it out, you two," Scott said, long used to their ways.

As Scott carried Alex up the steps, Valerie fixed a bright welcoming smile on her face. "How lovely to see you again, Alex," she cried, moving towards the head of the steps. "You know Edwina has been beside herself with excitement."

"How are you, Valerie?" Alex responded, seeing Valerie's hidden anger all too clearly.

"I'm very well." Valerie laid her hand possessively along Scott's tanned cheek. "How are *you*, darling?" she said softly. Just the two of them. "Flying back and forth must be one heck of a grind."

Wyn thought that unpardonable but Scott only shrugged. "No problem. I enjoy flying. Always have. I don't know about Alex, though. Having a leg in plaster makes the going tough."

"At least she didn't have to limp home." Valerie's voice was smooth and teasing even if the sight of Alex cradled in Scott's strong arms was raising her blood pressure.

They looked too comfortable with each other; their bodies too much at ease as though they knew intimately one another's flesh. Valerie had to wrestle with unbidden images that sprang so vividly into her mind. She had confidently expected to see the bewitching ballerina reduced to mere mortal status, awkward with her crutches. Instead, Scott had obviously taken to carrying her around like a national treasure. Too much of that, Valerie thought, and I'll be eaten up with acid rage.

Now it was the housekeeper's turn to rush out onto the veranda, arms outstretched, crying out with joy.

God, how tedious! Valerie thought. No one has ever put on this kind of welcome for me. Being on hand for the homecoming mightn't have been such a good idea after all.

She was left all by herself, feigning nonchalance as Scott carried Alex into the house to let her freshen up before the special afternoon tea Ella had prepared. All of them so excited.

Except Scott.

That alone gave Valerie tremendous heart.

Valerie took great care with her dressing for dinner, donning a sexy little shift dress in white crepe, simple but dynamite with her figure. She had shampooed her hair, as well, not that it really needed it. Now it fell just clear of her shoulders in a shining curtain with plenty of body. Silver earrings for a bit of sparkle, three bangles, pewter slingbacks to set off her enviable long legs. Scott liked the way she always looked good. Another quick spray of Saint Laurent's Opium and Valerie had physical and mental balance back on track.

Scott was an extremely active man with wonderful health. Darling Alex with her poor little leg in plaster would most certainly be housebound, stuck on a sofa. Valerie planned on riding out with Scott the next day. Born and bred on a sheep station, she was an excellent horsewoman and she knew she looked super in figure-hugging riding clothes.

Valerie took a quick look around her guest bedroom, large by any standards and furnished with a mixture of colonial grandeur and relaxed informality. The colour scheme was light and airy, a rich cream and white; even the original dark furniture was painted. But she was fed up with the fact that *darling Alex's* old room, refurbished exquisitely for her seventeenth birthday, had been kept empty. Like a shrine. Valerie had almost got to the point where she was going to discuss it with Scott but wisely thought better of it.

She adored this house, so very different from her parents' modern ranch style, but then the Freemans made no claims to founding a pastoral dynasty. They were latecomers on the scene. Main Royal homestead was a real mansion warmed by sumptuous things, every last one of them collectors' pieces. As wealthy as her own family was, Valerie always felt a sense of privilege when she walked through the front door.

When she'd been younger she had never aspired to attracting the attention of the devastatingly handsome Scott McLaren, one very good reason being he was known to be madly in love with his aunt's ward, but when the big love affair crashed on the rocks, Valerie seized an outstanding opportunity to move up in the world. She started to frequent all the polo matches where Scott and his team played, winning more often than not, and became a groupie in the process.

She wasn't the only woman after him. *No way!* But she had more stamina than most and knew how to exploit situations. In other words, how to get rid of the competition. After all, her mother had told her, it would be the greatest coup of their lives if she could land Scott McLaren.

Things had been going quite well until *darling Alex* popped up.

She found everyone in what Edwina persisted in calling the conservatory. Certainly there were many magnificent plants, soaring golden canes and huge, luxuriant ferns. It boasted a lofty window wall, a marble floor and central fountain, but to Valerie's mind it was far too luxurious to be called simply a conservatory. Who would put an antique Baccarat chandelier in a garden room, for God's sake? Or a massive baronial fireplace, in summer filled with flowering plants?

"A martini would be lovely," she said with a smile, buoyed up by her sexy look. Scott was indescribably attractive to her. *Darling Alex* was seated on one of the sofas, Edwina beside her, both women smiling softly. How wonderful they looked. *Perfect*. Edwina McLaren in her early sixties was remarkably well preserved, her figure slim, her skin unlined, thick wavy hair arranged elegantly around her patrician face. She should really have it coloured, Valerie thought, but then it would take far too much attention.

Darling Alex instead of looking wan and pale was breathtaking in some sort of gold silk caftan subtly embroidered with gold thread and tiny topaz stones. The cast wasn't in evidence. Valerie had to hand it to her. She certainly knew how to get herself together. Maybe a touch theatrical. Why not? When her knee healed and Valerie had taken to saying nightly prayers, Alexandra Ashton could return to her life on the stage.

Both Wyn and Alex sitting so quietly were aware of the quality of Valerie's bright, hard scrutiny. Both were essentially kind-hearted, deeply courteous women. Valerie was a guest, albeit uninvited, but so far as they knew, in serious contention for the role of mistress of Main Royal. Valerie was a force in her own right. Alex could have wept with the knowledge but she had done it all to herself.

Valerie scintillated over dinner, clearly triumphant at being seated to Scott's right.

I'm being put in my place, Alex thought, trying not

to be bothered at all. She had to accept that Scott had moved on even if she couldn't believe he would settle for a woman like Valerie. Valerie was striking, confident, entertaining over dinner even if the conversation was mostly gossip and largely excluded Alex, but there was no actual *warmth* in her.

She frequently touched Scott's hand or arm with the ease of long familiarity while he added point and depth to her stories with a few simple truths or sharp observations. Scott was never prepared to go along with hearsay, Alex knew. Neither was he one for passing on gossip but he smiled on Valerie and let her sparkle.

"So what about you, Alex?" Valerie finally spared her a moment, looking across the gleaming table exquisitely set with silver, bone china and crystal that would make anyone gasp. "Don't think you and Victor Dreyer are fooling the public." Her voice was arch. "You look so wonderful onstage together, the rapport *must* spill over into real life."

Are you crazy? Alex thought. "Victor and I are good friends, Valerie. Nothing more."

"The standard answer yet again. Has she confided in you, Edwina?" Valerie teased.

"Not everything." Wyn kept her tone light. "But I don't think Victor is to Alex's taste."

"I've heard *that* before," Valerie said smirking. "He's very handsome." She hesitated a moment, then laughed. "He's not gay, is he, darling?"

Alex drew a deep breath. "I couldn't say, but he's entitled to his privacy like everyone else."

Valerie's eyes flickered. "Of course. But he does have a rare gift for conveying passion, you must agree. I saw you together in *Romeo and Juliet*. It was impossible to look away from you. There was so much *feeling*!"

"Acting, Val," Scott said in a dry voice. He glanced

at Alex, his attitude very much Big Brother. "It's high time you took another bite."

"I thought I was doing quite well." Alex dutifully forked a small mouthful of roast fillet of beef. It was wonderfully tender and flavoursome, served with a delicious avocado bearnaise and vegetable accompaniments, but she had little appetite. There was something quite unnerving in Valerie's bright stare.

"I hope you're not one of those dancers affected by anorexia?" Valerie tutted, her expression pitying. "I read a terrible story about an American ballerina—"

"Yes, I know the one you mean—" Alex laid down her knife and fork "—but I don't have to diet to keep weight off, Valerie. The difficulty is keeping it on."

"Another few mouthfuls and you'll be doing fine," Scott said, nodding encouragement.

"You should stop hassling me." Alex shook her head.

"I thought I was showing my concern," he said in a dry murmur.

Their voices weren't confrontational. It was more a familiar exchange. Valerie *hated* it. "You should have that plaster off in another month, Alex," she consoled. The quicker the better, she thought. Get rid of her. Valerie could see Scott's eyes. The intolerable kindling in them when he looked at the girl.

"With any luck." Alex lifted her head, the light from the candles in the tall candelabrum striking her hair like fire.

"You were very fortunate to have had Ian Tomlinson," Valerie pointed out almost severely, then could have cursed herself.

"How did you know that, Val?"

How did she indeed? She had never mentioned visiting Alex in the hospital. Stalling for time, Valerie picked up her long-stemmed wineglass and sipped the fine

Cabernet. "Surely one of you told me?" She looked steadily around the table, bold in the manner of someone telling a downright lie. You idiot! she thought.

Wyn was very quiet for a moment. "*I* didn't," she said, shooting a troubled glance at Alex.

"It must have been me." Alex decided to let Valerie off the hook. "That's right, it was."

"I don't know when," Scott challenged, a faint edge to his voice. He stretched out a hand, turned Alex's averted face and looked at her. "I think you should have an early night. The flight seems to have drained your strength." In actual fact, her beauty took the breath out of him.

"Yes, darling," Wyn seconded. "Are you sure you're not in pain? You're very pale."

"Not at the moment," Alex said, smiling. "But I'll go quietly."

"When you're ready to retire, Scott can carry you to your room," Wyn said in her gentle voice. "We've ordered a wheelchair so you'll be more mobile. It should arrive tomorrow."

That's right, carry her around, Valerie thought savagely. In all her life she had never seen anyone so fragile without being in the least weak or waiflike. The look was more *romantic*. Even with her leg in plaster, Alexandra Ashton was incredibly graceful. It simply wasn't fair.

They were lingering after coffee in the drawing room when Scott suddenly bent and scooped Alex up.

"Oh, I'm sorry," she murmured in a dazed voice, showing her fatigue. "Was I drifting off?"

"You were." Scott's face was very close to hers, eyes glinting, mouth sensual.

"Don't feel guilty, darling." Wyn laughed and rose

from her armchair. "It's been a long day. I'll come and help you undress."

"Goodnight, Valerie," Alex called, uncomfortably aware that Valerie was so livid even her eyes were turning green.

"Night, Alex," Valerie responded, recrossing her long legs. "Sleep well."

"I won't be long, Val," Scott said, looking back to reassure her. "We might take a stroll around the compound. Work off that excellent dinner."

"Lovely!" Valerie was happy suddenly.

"Where are your pain-killers?" Wyn asked Alex when they reached her bedroom. "Will you need them?"

"I'm afraid so." Alex slumped back on the bed, one side of her body throbbing in sympathy with her leg. "They're in the cabinet in the bathroom."

"I'll get them, dear." Wyn moved off.

Scott stood quietly over Alex, his handsome face sombre, even brooding. "I didn't give you much time, did I?"

"True." Her heart quickened under that look. "You never did." She held his gaze, her eyes the exact match of the topaz stones that sparkled on her caftan.

He laughed a little harshly. "That's some trick with your eyes."

"Trick? Good Lord, how?" she countered.

"The soft dazzle. I suppose all witches have such eyes."

"I don't know that I believe in witches."

"I was betrayed by one. Now I know how to protect myself."

"I think you should go back to Valerie."

"I intend to." His expression changed again, became cool and glittery.

"The future Mrs Scott McLaren...?"

The silence seemed to stretch forever, then Scott turned away, speaking bluntly. "Why not? You didn't want the job."

Much later that night with a perfect full moon riding high over the towering sand-dunes and the air thrumming with an aboriginal chant that was part of her homecoming, Alex saw Valerie and Scott walking in the garden. The moon's silver radiance lit up Valerie's blond hair and her white dress so that she appeared all silver, a moon goddess, clinging to Scott's arm and murmuring into his ear.

Alex, who had been lying on the day bed in a cool, scented breeze streaming through the open French doors, tried to get up, to find a hiding place. Facing Scott's involvement with Valerie was the hardest thing she had ever known. She couldn't move easily; neither could she seem to turn away. Scott had turned Valerie to him. She was reaching up, placing one hand along his cheek.

Don't look, Alex thought. I'm not prepared for this. I'll never be. Only the radiance of the moon flooded the scene, sharply outlining the man and woman who came together.

Then she heard Valerie's voice, husky with yearning, saying, "Scott..."

It was a moan of desire.

Alex felt her cheeks burn with hot blood. Inside her darkened room, she found her crutches, grasped them firmly, then shoved them beneath her arms.

Dear God, Alex thought. What have I *done*? She had given up her great chance at happiness. She would never have it again.

CHAPTER SIX

TRUE to his promise, Scott spent very little time at the homestead, working from dawn to dusk and retiring to his study soon after dinner, where he told them he had a mountain of paperwork to get through before his trip to Japan. Alex had never known him so aloof and it distressed her though she did her level best to hide it. She might have known it would be this way.

Wyn was also affected. Apart from their terrible rift, Wyn had never seen Scott keep Alex at arm's length, but that's what he wanted, and Wyn's heart ached for both of them. The prospect of ever having Valerie in the family made Wyn miserable and nervous. Valerie's obvious attractions aside, she had a certain hardness of soul. If Scott married her, Wyn knew her days at Main Royal were numbered. Not that she saw that as unreasonable. Scott's wife would naturally want to be mistress in her own home, but Wyn had the dismal feeling that Valerie would somehow lock her out entirely and undoubtedly do it in such a way that Scott wouldn't be made aware of it. Alex Valerie viewed through a veil of enmity. Wyn was quite sure once Valerie was mistress of Main Royal, Alex would never set foot on it again.

It was easier when Scott went away and Alex and her godmother slid into the loving closeness they had enjoyed for so many years. Each took a genuine delight in the other's company and they had the freedom to discuss every topic under the sun. It was a perfect, peaceful two weeks that stretched into three as Scott was delayed with additional business. Alex was eating and sleeping better, both women taking advantage of Abe's familiar presence to drive them anywhere on the station they wished to go. Often they went on picnics—"billabong buffets"— as Wyn called them.

Scott came home at last, astonishingly vivid. Alex's heart leapt like a bird at the sight of him, soaring, soaring, lifting clear of her body. He hugged and kissed Wyn before finally dropping a kiss on her cheek.

"You look vastly better." His eyes moved over her so imperiously it took Alex all her willpower to retain her composure. Why did he look at her like that? It was as though nothing had changed. There was the same blaze though she was unaccustomed to the remoteness of his tone. It had to be he never tired of her looks, but she could see he no longer trusted her.

When it was time for the plaster to be removed, Scott flew Alex back to Sydney for her appointment with Ian Tomlinson, her orthopaedic surgeon, asking and receiving permission to be with her when the cast came off. Alex had never talked about what would happen if the delicate surgery wasn't successful, but he knew behind the quiet stoicism she had to be churning inside. Suddenly he was overpoweringly aware of her celebrated position in her own world. She was a moving, marvellous dancer. She had reached the top not only through her technical brilliance but because it was allied to back-breaking hard work. A crucial moment was coming up. Would Alex dance again? No matter what he had suffered through her rejection, he couldn't forget he had once sworn to love her until the sun dimmed in the sky.

When Alex eventually saw her leg free of plaster, she thought for a moment she would burst into tears. Scott must have thought so, too, because he reached for her hand and held it firmly. She was shocked at how white and weak the limb looked, but after an examination conducted in silence with an intense frown between his bushy brows, Ian Tomlinson finally looked back at her with an almost cheerful smile.

"Good, good," he said, nodding. "I'll need an X-ray, but unless I'm very much mistaken and I haven't been in many long years, the leg's looking fine. I'm not making any rash promises, I don't want to get your hopes up only to have them dashed, but things are looking better than I first thought. Obviously you're wonderfully fit. You're young and a good healer. You have everything going for you."

"What exactly is Alex's therapy?" Scott asked, thinking her expression, for all the doctor's words, was stricken. "I need to know because I'll be taking her back to Main Royal to recuperate."

Ian Tomlinson peered over spectacles that slid continually down his nose. "A splendid mansion, too. I've been looking at it for years. It's on the cover of one of my wife's coffee-table books. Do you have a swimming pool along with all the billabongs?" he half joked.

"We do," Scott affirmed. "Alex will have the use of that. There's nothing we can't get for her if she needs it."

"I'm sure," The consultant answered a little dryly, scribbling something additional in his notes. "Hydrotherapy is essential and must be commenced right away. In two or three days she'll need the services of a physiotherapist who's used to working with dancers. How do we go there?" He glanced up.

Scott made a wry face. "We had a woman lined up but she cried off at the last moment. Maybe she thought she'd be too isolated. We're still on the track. Something will be arranged. I promise."

Ian Tomlinson looked thoughtful. "Now I might be

able to help you there. A colleague's nephew, nice young fellow, highly regarded, works with gymnasts and dancers, is wanting a few months off to look around. I should think he would like nothing more than a stint in the Outback if you could put him up.''

Scott glanced quickly at Alex as if he didn't much like the idea. ''Wouldn't you prefer a woman?''

''Actually I don't mind,'' Alex said truthfully, little beads of perspiration breaking out at her temples. From the condition of her leg, it didn't look as though she would be whipping out any fouettés, much less putting on her pointe shoes, for a long, long time. Her decision to become a dancer had demanded so much of her, not just incredibly hard work, but even more, the loss of her only love. Now there were no guarantees she would ever dance again.

''Alex?'' There was a concerned note in Scott's voice. He put his hand lightly on her shoulder and felt the trembling right through her body.

''I'm sorry.'' She put strength into her voice. ''I was only thinking a man would be out and about most of the time, seeing as much as he could of the station and station life. A woman might want perhaps to be entertained in her off hours.''

Scott considered that, thinking it highly probable. ''It's entirely up to you, that's if Mr Tomlinson *is* able to help us out.''

''I'll most certainly try,'' the consultant returned, his attitude that of a man determined to get results. ''Here, let me put through a call.''

The result of that phone call was that Peter Somerville accompanied them back to Main Royal the following day, his demeanour suggesting this was the chance of a lifetime. On first meeting Alex and Scott at the light aircraft terminal, he told Alex he had once seen her

MARGARET WAY 99

dance the Dying Swan and found her performance heart-breaking.

"In fact, my girlfriend cried her eyes out," he added. "Believe me, Miss Ashton, I'm going to do everything in my power to see you get back to your career." There was a tremendous concentration of earnestness and admiration in the young man's eyes.

Alex liked him at once. She wasn't sure about Scott. His manner was brisk, bordering on clipped. Peter Somerville was a fair-haired, blue-eyed young man, not tall but compact and strong, with an open, relaxed expression and a kind, attractive smile. Alex thought they would do very well together. She had needed the services of physiotherapists in the past, both male and female, and Mr Tomlinson had assured her that Peter was known for his excellent results.

That first night back on Main Royal, Peter joined them for dinner. It was Wyn who decided Peter would stay at the homestead instead of in one of the self-contained bungalows just outside the main compound. He was obviously a well-bred young man, successful in his chosen profession, and his easy, friendly manner had an instant appeal. Apart from that, Wyn realised full well the tension between Scott and Alex was still firmly in place. So far as Wyn was concerned, Peter Somerville's presence smoothed the strong currents that swirled and eddied around them.

Unlike Wyn who always responded to pleasant and attractive young people, McLaren felt his nerves tightening every time Somerville's blue eyes turned in Alex's direction, which they did too often as far as he was concerned. Without question, Somerville was responding to the powerful woman magic Alex was able to summon up so effortlessly.

Although Somerville had spoken several times about

a girlfriend (Kate was her name; they'd been going together for about seven or eight months), McLaren, who had him under close scrutiny, realised that Alex in a few hours had come to represent everything that was graceful and beautiful in a woman. Although he couldn't help liking the guy, his susceptibility to Alex had already begun to grate.

If it had been McLaren's choice, or Janet Dalton had kept to her end of the agreement, Alex would have had a female physiotherapist to attend to her program. Fewer complications with a woman, he reasoned. Alex would still be needing the wheelchair until her leg strengthened sufficiently to bear her full weight, anything up to ten days, but instead of detracting from her mystique, the added vulnerability made her a creature of human fragility as well as flame.

Later in the evening, McLaren excused himself while the others retired to the library to listen to some new CDs he had brought back for Wyn—piano and violin favourites, an album of world opera and Sting's latest. Wyn had catholic tastes. When he returned to the library sometime after ten, he found them all in a companionable silence listening to the great Spanish soprano, Monserrat Caballe, singing an aria from *La Bohème*.

"Oh, hello there, darling." Wyn lifted her head from the back of her wing chair. "Come and relax. You push yourself too hard."

"I might have a nightcap at that." McLaren walked to a small rosewood table that held a selection of glasses and decanters filled with spirits. "Anyone join me?" He glanced back, noting that Alex looked dreamy and drowsy after the long flight.

"Thank you, no." Peter Somerville sprang up immediately as though on cue. "I thoroughly enjoyed this evening but I mustn't intrude any longer."

"Peter, you're not intruding at all," Wyn protested. "You mustn't feel like that."

"No indeed. We need to keep you happy," McLaren commented with his white, charm-the-birds-out-of-the-trees smile. "Alex's speedy recovery is very important to us all."

"I quite realise that," Peter hastened to respond. "I look on my appointment as an honour and a challenge."

He knew Alex was Miss McLaren's ward, but what was her *exact* relationship to McLaren? Now that was the tricky one. There was a strange intensity between the two of them that had even engulfed him. Handsome as the devil, rich and powerful, in the grandeur of his own setting, McLaren appeared even more formidable than he had at the airport. Peter felt he would have to pull out all the stops to pass muster.

"We'll begin hydrotherapy in the morning, Miss Ashton," he said, although she had asked him to call her Alex. "It'll be a couple of days before we start on specific exercises."

"I'll be ready, Peter." She gave him the smile that held him in a web of enchantment. He had never met anyone like Alexandra Ashton in his entire life.

"What a nice young man," Wyn sighed happily after Peter had gone. I just know he's going to fit in. Alex tells me he comes with her consultant's recommendation, Scott."

"I don't know that he exactly comes with mine," McLaren said in a dry voice. "It can't have escaped your attention, Wyn, that he finds Alex fascinating." Although he smiled, his eyes were as hard and brilliant as jewels.

Wyn caught the gleam; realised her beloved nephew couldn't let go of Alex any more than she could let go of him. The bond went too deep. "Ah well, darling," she said soothingly, "Alex has been turning heads since she was a baby. I'm sure Peter won't lose sight of the reason he's here."

"Besides, he's got a girlfriend," Alex added, distractedly touching a hand to her temple. "The main thing is he's good at his job." She leaned forward and lifted the hem of the floral skirt she wore with a simple halter-neck top. "Doesn't look too good at the moment, does it?" She ran a soothing hand from her knee to her ankle. "I knew almost the moment I took off for that fish dive, I was going to suffer an injury. Strange, isn't it? A kind of premonition of disaster. It would never have happened with Victor, but Michael hasn't partnered me often. He doesn't have Victor's strength or experience. I was in the right place. He wasn't."

"Well, you certainly paid for it," McLaren commented, his voice full of muted anger. "Your leg looks frail now, but it will be a different story in another month. You're amazingly strong for all that look of fragility."

"Yes, Alex." Wyn added her encouragement. "Your rate of recovery has always been very fast."

"I've never been injured like this, Wyn," Alex said simply. "Even if I heal well, that doesn't mean I'll dance again. Or dance at *my* level. When I think of the constant changes of direction, the pivoting, *en pointe*, leaping, coming down hard on the leg... My knee could very easily give way. I could twist it very badly again."

They could see that this might be so. "Let's take each day as it comes, Alex," McLaren advised. "Tomlinson sounded optimistic. If anyone can get right, you can."

"I wish it were that easy," Alex sighed, then a look of optimism came into her face. "I'm a little tired now. That's why I'm feeling sorry for myself. I'll be much better tomorrow."

"So does that mean you're ready for bed?" McLaren tossed off the rest of his Scotch.

"Not before I take another look at the night sky," Alex said. "I've missed it. One doesn't see skies like ours anywhere else in the world. So vast, so free of anything else."

"Then we'll have to go out on the veranda." McLaren rose to his feet, close-up snapshots of the young Alex filling his mind. Alex had soaked up aboriginal culture, from their rituals and dances to their great herbal knowledge. Most of all, she had loved the wonderful stories of the Dreamtime. There were stories for everything—the cycle of life, death and the spirit world, earth, fire and water, the sun, moon and stars. Growing up, she had listened with fascination to a great variety of myths. Often she had asked him to lift her higher on his shoulder so she could pluck down one of the "diamond apples" that hung from the sky.

Alex saw things as he did. Or so he had believed.

He looked down at her lying back on the sofa. She looked incredibly beguiling in the way that she had, a magical balance between innocence and sexuality. The fabric of her top cupped her delicate breasts like a second skin. The fluid skirt outlined her lithe, slim body. This was going to be one hell of a rough time for him, he thought. A test of his resolve. Without the plaster cast, he was carrying her higher, closer. It set up a confusion of emotions in him, a sexual hostility he couldn't deny, while his blood ran like molten lava. His physical reactions were the same even if his mind wasn't. The old thrill remained and he had to deal with it.

"If it's all right with you two, I'll turn in." Wyn stood up, gently smothering a contrived yawn. "Are you sure you don't need me, Alex?"

"You toddle off," Alex told her in an affectionate voice. "I've got to get myself mobile."

"You'd better remember it has to be gradual." McLaren scooped her up much as he would a child. "Straining will only put you back."

"I know." Held so close, Alex felt the soft beat of wings start up in her breast.

"I'll see her to her room, Wyn," Scott assured his aunt. "I don't know about helping her with her nightie, though."

"Certainly not." Alex managed to sound casual even when sensation upon sensation was claiming her. Every atom of her body strained to meld with his.

Scott carried her out onto the veranda, not lowering her into an armchair as she expected but moving out towards the balustrade.

"You don't mean to throw me over?" she half joked, aware he was in a dangerous mood.

The starlight, luminous, unearthly, glinted in his eyes. "Alex, I could break you in two."

"I'm sure you could." She stared back at him, too vulnerable for all this. "It goes deep with you, doesn't it?"

"And don't you forget it."

"Not with you reminding me all the time. You surely can't hate me?"

"Shouldn't I?" His body ached with the restraint of not making love to her. An agony of want. By now he had to know it was permanent.

"I didn't commit a crime," she said.

"You did *against me*." He gave a bleak laugh, setting her down on the wide railing where it made a juncture with a soaring white column. He curled his arms around her, something he had done countless times in the past.

"But you're all right now." The charge burned like

acid. She tried to talk her way out of it. "You have Valerie. I'm thinking of her."

"What, deep down here?" His hand slid deliberately, provocatively, over her breast, his fingers pressing into an area over her heart so she was barely able to contain her anguish. "Does my having Valerie let you off the hook?"

"Apparently not. You can't forgive me my old sins. But I want you to be happy, Scott."

"Happy?" His tone was derisive. "What the hell are you talking about?"

"Then what *is* Valerie to you?" she demanded in some consternation. "Have you slept with her?" Suddenly she pictured it. Drove it away.

"It might sound strange to you, Alex, but that's none of your business."

She drooped her head. "Of course you have. Sex is important to you."

"Hell, yes. It's much too early to give it up. You're not going to try to tell me it's not in *your* nature. Not my little Alex. Not the girl who used to go wild in my arms."

"Maybe I've grown used to love," she said in a soft, saddened voice. "Sex is a passing satisfaction. Love is a miracle."

"And you found it and gave it away." His voice held grief as well as contempt, giving her an insight into the dashing of his hopes and dreams, his trust, already badly eroded by his mother's defection.

"You won't understand, will you?" she said bleakly. "You *can't*. A door opened to me. I had to walk through."

"Okay! I can understand that," he retorted in an impassioned voice, "but was it the right door? You had a dream but you didn't let me in on it. You didn't tell *me*.

You didn't once say I want a career on the bloody stage, Scott. Instead you told me we were going to be together. For always. That nothing could ever part us."

It seemed incredibly strange now but it was true. She had wanted a foot in both worlds. He had forced her to choose but she had never found fulfilment in her choice. Or solace. "Please, Scott, no more. I'm so sad."

He gazed up at the blossoming stars, trying to calm himself. How could he hold such bitterness and anguish in his heart when his whole body was aflame with desire. He wanted to lift her, carry her off...

Memories surged so sweet and powerful, for a moment he felt disoriented, spinning out into the past. He could smell the native boronia with its unforgettable heady fragrance, the boronia of the bushland. At the same time, images began to appear, sharp and clear. He held his breath.

"Scott, darling." It was Alex, her voice soft and shaken, her face and body washed white by the moonlight and the radiance of a billion stars.

They were together in their secret place, so silent, so perfect, an enchanted spot reached only by a narrow, overgrown tunnel of feathery acacias that discharged soft golden blossoms on their heads and shoulders. The almost circular desert pool was pure and clean, very like mineral water, very deep at the centre, surrounded by a wide margin of white sand edged with marvellously smooth boulders, polished in their perfection, great and small.

He hadn't been there for two years or more so intimately was the pool linked with Alex in his mind....

He could see her dreaming face, incandescent with the deep magic that flashed between them. He could feel her soft skin, her delicate bones, so fine, so silken to the touch. He could feel the same pounding desire and under the desire a soaring exultation. Once they had sheltered there in a great summer thunderstorm that broke unexpectedly. He remembered the monstrous, magnificent electrical display, Alex's high, excited laugh, almost drowned out by the clamour of the shrieking birds that crowded into the trees, flocks of them, heralding the storm. Then when the storm was over and the mirage-haunted heat was broken by great gusts of cooling fresh air, then...ah, then...

Nothing but nothing could dim his memories or the knife-keen pain of loss never fully realised until she had gone. He could never share those utterly perfect early days with Alex again. They belonged to another time.

Now he held her back against him, trying, without succeeding, to harden his heart against her. It was a measure of his vulnerability. No pain. No gain. He could pity his former self.

"Alex, you'll mend," he offered eventually. No matter how she had wrecked his life, a good life, a life that was exactly what he wanted, it was empty without the one single human being.

"You'll do perfect fouettés or whatever they're called," he promised. "It's even possible I'll come to see your triumphant return to the stage. Dancers of your calibre need their adoring public. But I need a wife to hold in my arms. A wife to be always by my side. A woman to give me children. Immortality, if you like, the continuation of our heritage. The very last thing in this world I want is a woman who's never there."

On the morning of the fifth day, Alex found to her delight she could do without her crutches. Ian Tomlinson had made no error of judgment sending Peter to her. He was a gifted physiotherapist, his program of hydrotherapy allied to an expanding series of balletic-type exercises hastening her rate of recovery. Both of them were fully aware no real strain could be placed on her knee but the leg was quickly regaining movement and strength.

"Alex, for goodness' sake!" Wyn started to her feet when Alex walked unaided into the breakfast room, her expression delighted.

Scott, who had just returned to the house from a dawn start, turned from the sideboard to look at her. "What did I tell you? Want a thing badly enough and you can make it happen. Congratulations, Alexandra."

"A long way to go yet," she said, smiling at him radiantly. "But it ain't bad."

"Darling, it's wonderful!" Wyn had tears in her eyes.

"This girl is some kind of genius," Scott mocked. "Make no mistake, she'll be pirouetting around the house in under a month."

"Peter's played a big part in this," Alex said happily. "Where is he anyway? He always beats me into breakfast."

"Taking a quick shower." Scott began to help himself to bacon, sausages and eggs. He came out riding with me this morning so he could learn more about station life. I'm afraid he took a bit of a fall. A fraction slow in ducking his head under a branch."

"But he's all right?" Concern echoed in Alex's voice.

"Sure." Scott laid down a serving fork, his tone a mite terse. "Now, what can I get you, Miss Ashton?"

She came to stand at his shoulder, not even reaching it. "I'll have an orange juice and some pawpaw, thanks."

"Nothing else?" He glanced down at her, happiness and relief visible in every singing line of her body.

"It's all I need, you know. I'm not a big man running a station."

"You could still do with a few pounds and you just

might be able to ride out with me sometime." He poured the orange juice, handed it to her.

"Oh, that will be wonderful. I can't wait!" She threw up her head, reminding him of her enthusiasm when she was a young girl. "I want to gallop. I want Sun Dance, your swiftest colt. I want to see the birds, the budgies and the parrots, scores of them flying in a riot of brilliant colours over our heads."

"Not so fast, Alex," Wyn said, laughing. "We have to take care of you."

"There's a polo match on Carinda next weekend," Scott said. "You might be able to make that."

Alex's topaz eyes filled with pleasure. "I don't see why not." She sat down at the table beside Wyn. "You're playing?" she asked Scott.

"Of course." He glanced at her excited face. She wasn't wearing make-up. The glow in her cheeks was quite enough. The glorious mane of her hair shone like a halo around her face and fell over her shoulders. "I had to give up captaining the team," he explained. "I simply couldn't afford the time or the commitment. Jake O'Connell's in charge now. He's more or less turned professional. On the circuit. It should be a good day. I'm looking forward to it."

"Can we take Peter?" Alex asked. "He's sure to enjoy it."

"I've no objection," Scott said dryly and glanced pointedly at his aunt. "He might take his eyes off you for a change and watch the horses."

CHAPTER SEVEN

ALEX sat back in her striped canvas chair, letting her eyes roam over the polo fields. The flat grasslands of Carinda Station spread away in all directions, the myriad colours shimmering and changing with the wind. It was a beautiful day, the sky a deep smouldering blue, cloudless except for the shadows of coasting eagles and falcons flitting across the sun. All around the perimeter of the field lending shade were bauhinias in bloom, sending down showers of pink, white and cerise orchidlike flowers. Alex found the sight entrancing, stroking one perfect pink blossom under her chin. There were stands too of limewood, wild pear and the native fig with its dark purplish fruit.

A sweet-scented breeze was blowing across the field, coming right at her. She drew the fresh clean air into her lungs, conscious of the relaxation of her limbs and a deep feeling of warmth and well-being. There was excitement, as well, because she and the enthusiastic crowd circling the grounds had come some considerable distance to attend, either by light aircraft or road to see the fastest game in the world.

Polo.

It was hard to believe the game had been played in Persia as long ago as 600 B.C., brought to the Western world by British cavalry officers returning from India's north-west frontier. Scott's great-grandfather had tried not too successfully to establish a team as early as the 1870s, but it wasn't until Scott's grandfather returned from the Second World War and began to breed the

110

finest polo ponies in the country that the game really
took off.

Main Royal's sires and dams were thoroughbred stock
and in constant demand both domestically and in India.
Climate, terrain and environment were ideal for the
game and every Outback station had ample room for any
number of polo fields. Players were out all year round
revelling in the sport that depended so heavily on the
courage and speed of their beloved horses. Scott was
marvellous to watch, hawk-eyed, fearless, with a wide
repertoire of strokes. His game was a combination of
physical strength and finesse. ''The spectator's dream'',
a visiting Indian maharani had called him, ''a magnificent peacock''.

Alex smiled as she thought of it. The gear alone was
glamorous and Scott was not only handsome, he possessed a splendid physique and effortless, stylish horsemanship. A lot of women Alex knew had all but devoted
their lives to watching Scott McLaren play polo. None
more than Valerie Freeman who was holding court with
her cronies some distance away.

Picnics were the order of the day, each group setting
up tables and chairs to accommodate a wide variety of
delicious food laid on by their hosts. There was quite a
bit of drinking at these meetings, as well. Alex expected
the champagne corks would start popping fairly soon.
She didn't care to drink herself in the heat of the day.
Even one glass of wine made her feel sluggish. She
would settle for coffee or a soft drink.

Wyn hadn't come. At the last minute she had decided
she couldn't really spare the time. The deadline for the
latest book was looming. Peter had been delighted to go
instead. He was talking to some newly found friends
over near one of the rigs. A few of the players were
warming up on the field, Scott among them. Alex

thought, as she often did, that he should be the model for the perfect equestrian statue.

She gave a long, relaxed sigh. She was feeling so much better. Almost her old self. She glanced down at her leg, tanned a light gold from short periods in the sun. The limb was looking good from her work-outs though she still wasn't able to put any strain on it. She was wearing a safari-type sleeveless shirt and matching above-the-knee shorts in a swirl of cream, bronze and tangerine cotton, a wide-brimmed straw hat on her head. All of the women who attended these matches put in quite an effort to look good while they watched their heroes thunder up and down the field, each endeavouring to eliminate his opposite number.

Sometimes when the calibre of the players wasn't terribly good, play could degenerate into a rough-house. Fortunately the two teams assembled today were not only excellent players but superbly mounted, as well. It promised to be exciting and Alex had her fingers crossed that there wouldn't be any bad spills.

When Valerie saw Alex briefly alone, she made a bee-line towards her, determined to reinforce her position. Most of the crowd today knew Alex. Indeed, they had given her a welcome befitting royalty, surging towards her all smiles and warm enquiries after her health. Valerie had had to keep her sunglasses on so she could shield the expression in her eyes from her friends. Alexandra Ashton was nothing less than a major threat.

"Hi there," she called brightly, causing Alex to turn her tawny head. "You look nice and relaxed."

"Oh, I am." Alex glanced up, admiring Valerie's cool, glamorous appearance in a multicoloured silk shirt and linen pants. "The bauhinias are filling the air with light."

"Actually I find them a bit of a nuisance," Valerie

said, slipping into the foldaway chair beside Alex. "So how are you feeling?" She subjected Alex to a long stare. "I must say you look very much better than the last time I saw you."

"I feel better, Valerie. Thank you. Peter has me on a fairly intensive program now. My leg is gaining strength and mobility every day."

"I'm absolutely thrilled for you." Valerie shot Alex a piercing look. "I know how anxious you must be to get back to your career."

"Well…that could be a long way off. If ever." Alex sighed as a sense of fatalism stole over her.

"You're joking, surely?"

Alex didn't much like Valerie's tone. "No. You must realise many dancers and athletes have had their careers cut short through injury."

"But you're young. You're strong. Why, the leg looks healed." Valerie glanced pointedly at Alex's slender limbs. "For that matter, I can't even tell which leg is the injured one."

"I'm doing well, Valerie." Alex didn't enlighten her further. "But I have to be careful. Obviously I have to prepare myself for the possibility I'll never make principal dancer again."

"But that's awful. That's cruel," Valerie said indignantly, her expression unintentionally comic.

"The world is full of trauma and crisis," Alex said. "I won't be *crippled*. It's just under extreme stress my knee mightn't hold up. But enough of me." She looked at Valerie assessingly. "You look like you're facing some sort of crisis yourself."

"I'm not sure I understand you." Valerie frowned.

"I think you do," Alex replied.

Valerie made a snorting sound. "Well, I can tell

you—have told you—I don't want you disrupting my plans. I should warn you I'm not the best of losers.''

"Which means the sooner I pack my bags and go home the better.''

"Something like that. There's something about you that Scott for all his self-containment can't handle.'' Valerie was her old self now, caustic, confident.

"Don't forget we've been through the thickets of grief together,'' Alex warned. "We loved each other *totally*. For a time.'' She *still* did. Only Scott didn't.

Valerie gave a harsh laugh. "I'm glad you added that. Look, I know you're a marvel in your profession, Alex. An artist I admire. I don't want to insult you in any way, but I feel I have to make clear you're putting an intolerable strain on our relationship. Surely you understand that?''

"Do you want the truth, Valerie?'' Alex asked very seriously.

"Of course.''

"In that case, I should tell you your tactics are all wrong. You're *not* Scott's wife. Nor his fiancée. Moreover, there's no talk of an engagement.''

"Is that what Scott's told you?'' Valerie demanded, looking affronted.

"It's what I've gathered.''

"From Edwina, of course,'' Valerie retaliated. "I have great respect for Miss McLaren, but clearly her loyalty is to you.''

"Valerie, let me be brief. Scott no longer loves me. That should give you heart. If my leg is restored to full strength, I'll go back to my career.''

"Can you give me your word?'' Valerie was firm. "I want some commitment.''

"You'll have to be content with what I say, Valerie.''

"Scott would never tolerate a wife who lived apart

from him,'' Valerie said with a shrug. "He wants family, children, a mistress for Main Royal. He wants someone who's there for him. Not someone who's never around.''

"Don't you think after all I've been through that I don't know that?'' Alex asked simply.

"Just tell me *one* thing. Do you still love him?''

"Maybe we've both run out of love,'' Alex said, gazing out on the field to where Scott was taking strike, "but neither of us can break the bond. So far as I'm concerned, I'm bound to Scott forever.''

Valerie sat a moment in stark silence considering this. Her eyes were hooded, the line of her mouth bitter. "Then we're locked into a situation, are we?'' she demanded.

"You'd find the same difficulty with Scott.''

"You're *wrong*,'' Valerie snapped. "He wants to cut you out of his life so he can start clean.''

"So where does he look for happiness now, Valerie? You?''

"There's no one else.''

"How can you bear that? Don't you want a man who loves you with all his heart?''

"Listen, even in my wildest moments I never thought I was going to get that,'' Valerie said flatly. "I'm a climber, Alex. You must know something about that with your brilliant career. I want to be somebody.''

"To the best of my knowledge, you are.''

"A great catch is what I have in mind.'' Valerie gave an ironic smile.

"Not a good husband? A good father for your children?''

"Scott will be all that. A great *lover*, as well. He's fabulously rich. He has a proud heritage and he's as handsome as a movie star.''

"He also has a dark side,'' Alex warned.

"All the more exciting!" Valerie looked around. "We'll have to discontinue our conversation, fascinating as it is. Your physiotherapist friend is hurrying back to you. What is it about you that gets the guys in, Alex? I really want to know."

"I couldn't tell you. Perhaps you'd better speak to Scott."

"Hope I wasn't interrupting?" Peter asked as he slipped into the chair Valerie had vacated so abruptly.

"Not at all." Alex gave him a smile. "We're waiting on one more player, then the match can get going."

"Easy to see why Scott's the big drawcard. He's really something on a horse. I'm so glad I was able to come today. It's been a great experience all round. Meeting you..." He broke off as a magnificent vintage car entered the grounds. The hood was down and the driver and his glamorous woman companion were waving enthusiastically at all and sundry as they made their entrance. "Wow!" Peter exclaimed, standing up to get a better view.

"Leslie Darrow with his latest girlfriend," Alex said laconically. "A real show-off is Leslie. His family owns Glenfield Station but Leslie is mostly a gentleman of leisure. He keeps the car tucked away for special occasions. I just hope he doesn't do anything foolish and blare the horn. It could spook the horses."

Peter looked surprised. "I would have thought polo ponies were a pretty placid lot what with all the rigours of the game and polo sticks whirling past their ears."

"They are, generally speaking, but I've seen them spooked by just little things like champagne corks popping, mirrors flashing, minders falling off when they're backing them out of the rig. Children. It doesn't take much."

"I suppose not. Wonderful car." Peter moved a little

farther off. "It looks in tiptop condition, too. The paint-work is perfection."

A small crowd was moving towards the car and Peter with a backward smile and a wiggle of his fingers moved with them.

Obviously a vintage-car enthusiast, Alex thought in-dulgently, lying back.

In another second, all hell broke loose as the car mov-ing in slow motion suddenly came to a halt, backfiring so loudly it was like an explosion shattering the air. Alex looked up in consternation, silently cursing Leslie for his grandstanding. He should know better but he habitu-ally failed to see the more serious side of events.

Like now.

Some distance off where three horses had been stand-ing quietly, loosely tied to a rig, there was pandemo-nium. The middle horse reared as fright urged it into violent action. The other two, who had shown no real signs of concern, suddenly joined in as waves of em-pathy ran along their sides. The reins loosened and they were off. Even worse, they were heading in Alex's di-rection with spectators compelled to scatter madly to left and right. Tables and chairs went down like ninepins. The horses were running tight, hooves drumming into the sandy turf. There was no way of dealing with this. It was all happening too fast.

Alex made a vain attempt to get out of the low-slung chair, then another that brought her jarringly to her feet. She wasn't fragile or helpless any more, she reminded herself. She was in *danger*—in a perfect position to be run down. The bolting horses kept on coming. No one had been prepared for a stampede, nevertheless some of the men were making valiant attempts to control the mad flight. One man was struck a glancing blow that tossed him up in the air. There were swirls of dust and fallen leaves flying upwards like a mini-tornado. Alex moved off swiftly under compulsion, stumbled then recovered. She was aware of a sharp shooting pain in her side. Her leg was dragging, resenting the strain that was being placed on it.

She felt an icy shiver of fear down her spine at the loss of mobility. On the periphery of her vision, riders were galloping towards the scene. One rider separated himself from the rest, yelling her name with such fervour it was like a battle cry that rallied her diminishing resources.

Immediately she knew what to do. She might appear deceptively delicate, but her body, hands and arms were quite strong. She lurched out towards the rider, positioning herself for the moment when in a piece of superb horsemanship he leaned out of the saddle and in one spontaneous flow of motion scooped her up and hoisted her before him. All this without his mount, and showing all the heart and turn of speed it possessed on the polo field, breaking stride.

For some moments the dismayed crowd was stunned. One minute it had been expecting to witness a horrible accident; in the next it was enthralled by splendid horsemanship allied to a young woman's courage. If it hadn't been so heart-stoppingly scary, they might have enjoyed themselves.

When Scott lifted an arm to signal that Alex was all right, cheers and resounding waves of applause began to ring out. The mad flight of the polo ponies had been stopped, a terrible accident averted.

"McLaren!" the crowd roared.

"You did it, Scott!"

The roars of congratulations were followed by the ultimate sign of relief—loud collective nervous laughter.

"You all right?" Scott mouthed. Under the hard brim

of his navy-and-white polo hat, his aqua eyes blazed in a drawn face.

Life. Death. Survival. That's all there is, Alex thought.

She nodded, too scared to speak in case the pain in her leg caused her stomach to heave. She bit down hard on her lip, acutely aware of the anger and tension in Scott's strong body. He was holding her so tightly she thought he would crush her. She seemed to be shaking all over, a combination of jarring and a powerful adrenaline rush.

"Alex?" Scott demanded again, feeling close to breaking point. It was hell to discover again what Alex meant to him.

"Leave it be, Scott. It's over." Her voice was low and ragged.

"Is it by hell?" His words were tight with the effort of control. "That bloody fool Darrow. I'll kill him."

"Please, Scott, loosen your arm."

He did so immediately, leaning downwards so his cheek grazed hers. "Are you hurt?"

"I'm jolted but I'm all right." She tried for both their sakes to make light of it. Scott stirred up had a fierce volatility.

"What bloody use was your Peter?" he rasped. "He never made the slightest attempt to go to your aid."

"Oh, Scott, *please*." Alex leaned back against him. "It would have taken a brave man indeed to intervene. One man was knocked off his feet. I just hope he's all right. Peter knows nothing about horses."

"That doesn't excuse him in my book," Scott gritted. "His job is to look out for you."

"Don't work yourself up," Alex implored. "Peter took fright."

"I've a damn good mind to send him packing," Scott said in the same hard voice.

"So where does that leave me?"

"I'll find somebody else. Anyway, you're coming along in leaps and bounds. You all but flew to me back there."

Alex shook her head. "Training, that's all. Gathering in one's weight so the body can levitate." Briefly she turned her attention away from him. "There's Peter now. He looks quite upset." She nodded towards the low railing where Peter was standing with a group of people waiting for Scott to ride in.

"He has good reason to be."

"Don't be cruel, Scott," she pleaded. "For *me*."

In the end, McLaren kept his peace until Alex, assuring everyone she was quite all right, had been driven back to the Carinda homestead to freshen up and have a quiet cup of tea. Then he had a private word with Darrow first, then Peter. Darrow took what he had to say squarely on the chin, apologising profusely and promising never to bring his pride and joy close to a polo ground again; Peter blinked and looked away almost as though he was about to burst into tears.

"All I can say is that I would have helped her if I could have, Scott, but there was no time."

"I won't have it there was *nothing* you could do," McLaren retorted. "You should have gone to her. *I* know it. So do you."

Peter nodded. "I'm sorry," he said dully. "It was a test and I failed it. I know nothing about horses. It's all I can do to stay on one. No one else could stop them, either." He sought some mitigating excuse.

McLaren said bluntly, "Some *tried*. Your place was with Alex. She's your charge. At the first sign of trouble you should have moved to get her out of harm's way. She's far from mobile yet. It's a hard lesson but one you might remember for the future. Alex could have been run down."

Peter flushed. "Don't rub it in, Scott. I *know*. It was so close. But thank God there was you. Clearly I'm out of place here."

"Accidents happen *everywhere*, Peter," McLaren reminded him soberly. "And that's the truth."

Late that night after the household had retired, Alex found herself too churned up to sleep. Reaction, she supposed. A light massage had eased the ache in her leg, but the nerves along that side of her body were jumping. She needed something to soothe her. Music to send her off to sleep. There was a tape she particularly enjoyed— an arrangement of Lennon and McCartney songs for cello and strings. But where was her Walkman? She usually kept it in her bedside drawer.

What other place? She pushed the drawer back in, trying to think. Suddenly she remembered having it when she was doing her exercises in the games room where she and Peter worked. Poor Peter! He was feeling at fault and hating it. But he was out of his element, really. Trying to restrain horses was decidedly risky even for people used to working with them on a daily basis. If he'd had any thought to come to her aid sooner panic had obviously blotted the thought out. *Scott* would have acted, but then, Scott could handle anything. Taking care of people, of situations, was his life.

Alex picked up her satin robe and shrugged into it. One would think after such a day she would be able to fall asleep right away, but her mind and body were restless, overstimulated. An image flooded her mind—Scott thundering towards her, willing her to hear his unspoken thoughts. She had done it so often in the old days just as he had taken her up before him, the two of them dizzy with rapture, riding off to their secret haunt where a bellbird often serenaded them with its thrilling cello voice. Small wonder she was so addicted to that beautiful instrument.

As always, there were a few wall brackets left on in the corridors to light the way. Wyn, if she couldn't sleep, often returned to her study. Scott, if he had anything on his mind, prowled the house like a panther. Moonlight poured through the high arched windows, spilling onto the polished parquet floors and turning them a rich amber. From the hallway came the whirr of the grandfather clock as it struck the hour. One a.m.

"Can't sleep, Alex?" A voice said.

She whirled with a little cry, searching the soft darkness. "Where are you, for heaven's sake?" she whispered.

"Waiting for you."

For one moment, such excitement shook her she almost moaned. Perhaps she *did*. She still couldn't see him but she took a few steps towards his voice. "Scott?"

"You sound like a frightened bird."

"Where *are* you?" She turned around, responding to the different direction of his voice.

"Here, lover." He held her fast, his warm breath brushing her cheek fragrant with the finest cognac.

"For mercy's sake!" She put her arms over his, her words trailing away because he was holding her, enfolding her with a palpable passion.

"What are you doing out here anyway?" He bent his head into her neck, his mouth moving slowly, voluptuously, over the silken column.

"I couldn't sleep," Heat engulfed her, flashed through her veins as his hands moved with urgency over the fine bones and hollow of her shoulders. She closed her eyes, leaned back, allowing him to caress her, to turn her heart inside out. A deep sense told her he had been drinking too much. Only his body was guiding him, not his mind, but being back in his arms was so wonderful she surrendered to her own yearnings. As his hands continued to arouse her, she sank back helplessly against him, her legs giving way, until finally he swept her off her feet and carried her silently back through the house. She was too far gone to speak, to protest, though she knew what would happen...didn't care. She *loved* Scott. That was all.

In his room it seemed for a moment he was going to toss her onto his bed, but even then his ingrained sense of caring for her held. He put her down gently on the mattress, leaning over her, an arm on either side of her body.

"You look beautiful," he said, though the expression in his eyes was far from gentle. They blazed down on her.

"This isn't going to solve anything." Her voice was frayed.

"No, but it's a force, isn't it?"

"You've been drinking," she said carefully.

"So? Turned into a little wowser, as well?" There was a faintly bitter twist to his beautiful mouth. Very slowly, never taking his eyes off her, he straightened up, then turned back to the door, locked it.

She sat up quickly, flushed, overstimulated, the bedside lamp making a magical nimbus of light around her head. "This can't happen, Scott."

When there were torrents of passion dammed up in him? "Hell, Alex," he mocked, "don't be stupid. It was *always* going to happen. The only question was when." His tone was tight, ironic, yet full of turmoil. When would it subside? "You nearly got yourself trampled today."

"Well, I didn't." She made a small, agitated gesture with her arms, wonderfully graceful. "You were there, like you're always there."

"But that's my job in life, isn't it? Looking out for you."

"Don't make it sound like it's been forced on you."

"Well, I can't seem to give it up, even when we're bad for each other."

That hurt her terribly. "Are we?" she asked, her anguished feelings in her face.

"Put it another way." He came back to her, threw himself down on the bed beside her fully dressed. "I'm crazy about you. I mean literally *crazy* and not much to be done about it. Life is full of heartbreak. You go off and leave me, make your life elsewhere, yet you're in everything I do. Hell, girl, I've suffered so much! Only a fool would surrender to your brand of enchantment. I hate myself for being that fool. It's destroying my life."

The anger directed at her, his fiery pride—that was altogether too much for her. "Scott, don't say that!" She moved towards him frantically, pressing her body close. "I'll go away. I'll go away tomorrow. Is that what you want?"

He laughed discordantly. "If it would work. The hell of it is, it wouldn't change anything." He glanced down at her flushed face, saw her distress. "Come here to me." He lifted his arm so she could fit herself into his side. So long since he had lain with her. An eternity. Yesterday. "The minute you're able, you'll do what you did before. You'll go off. Back to your career. Your life with me was just make believe."

"No!"

The hand that had been playing with her hair suddenly tightened as he wound a long, glittering lock across his palm.

"What if I made you pregnant?" he asked harshly. "What if I played the same damn rotten game you women play on men? I want a child. *Our* child. It doesn't matter to me whether it's a boy or a girl. I want part of you. Part of me. That way I'll always get to keep you."

"And what about Valerie?" She turned up her face.

"Come on, Alex," he drawled, returning to stroking her hair. "Valerie offers nothing more than sex. Damn, I don't even *like* her."

"But you use her."

"Indeed I do," he said with self-contempt, "as she uses me. Valerie doesn't *love* me, Alex. She loves what she perceives I stand for. Valerie's one of those women who's always working her way up the ladder."

"So you don't mean to marry her?"

He shrugged. "Marrying her is an answer of sorts." When Alex was the only answer.

"Wouldn't it be an idea to *tell* her of your doubts?"

"I'm aiming to, Alex, as if it's any of your business," he said caustically. "I don't think Val will be all that surprised. I'm not much good with women. I made my choice, but look where it got me."

"*I* love you, Scott." She caught his hand convulsively. *My God, how I love you.*

"You mean you're offering me your body?"

"If you want it."

"Oh yes, I want it," he said with a fierce laugh, "but I'm not so far gone I'd trap you. That's not my style. Is it a good time or the wrong time? I sure don't want any rubber between us."

"We never cared in the old days." Both of them surrendering to a passion that overwhelmed them.

"We must have been mad," he said in a grave, brooding voice. "*I* must have been mad. A spell you laid on me, Alex."

"*More* than a spell." Unless spells caused its victims to go up in flames. "I want you, Scott," she said in an agonised voice, knowing he would reject her profound feelings. "You don't have to worry."

"Why, are you on a contraceptive all the time?" A flash of anger and pain showed in his eyes.

"No, I'm not, but I know my own body."

"So did I once," he said almost sadly. "I loved you so much. Flesh of my flesh. Bone of my bones. Mind, body, spirit formed into one." He lifted her above him and held her poised, staring into her luminous eyes. "I hope you don't think I'm going to be gentle."

"When were you ever?" she challenged, her blood singing in her veins.

"Lord knows I tried." He gave a deep sigh, brought her down to him, revelling in the exquisite weight of her body on top of his, the silken warmth. "Alex, my torment."

He wasn't dreaming this. It was happening. He caught up her mouth, his hand clamped to the back of her head. Did a woman ever fully understand the driving urgency of a man's passion? The primitive need to know one special woman's body, to possess it? Sometimes, like now, it was an ungovernable desire sweeping aside all impediment.

"Let's get rid of this." He rolled her onto her back, peeling off her satin robe and flinging it to the end of the big four-poster, where it pooled for a moment before sliding to the Persian rug.

The nightgown went next, exposing her delicate woman's body so wondrously designed for a man's loving. Glowing in the low light, her skin was extraordinary, flawless, with the soft translucence of a pearl. White heat shot through his stomach. It was an agony only she could release.

"Alex, you're so fragile," he said. Undressed, she seemed tremendously vulnerable.

"No, I'm not!" She was half-afraid he would draw back.

"Well, you look it." His eyes devoured her as he spoke. "Next to you again. I don't know if I'm glad or plain mad."

"Surely just human," she breathed, her whole body atremble as though a million feathers were being brushed sensually across her skin. "There are worse things than wanting me, Scott."

"Then I'll have to wait until I'm dead to find out." His hand began caressing her with a highly sensuous yet devout hunger, moving from shoulder to breast, while he watched her body move convulsively. Such a deeply indented waist. He was certain he could put his hands around it. Delicate hips, satin thighs...

She reached out for him, in her frenzy ripping a button from his linen shirt. What he was doing to her was excruciating, yet he lifted himself away. Stood up.

"Scott?" Her voice betrayed her. Taut, a little frightened.

"*I* choose the time, my love." Even as he said it, he was tugging at his shirt, unzipping his jeans, standing momentarily in brief navy hipsters.

His body was magnificent with a sculptured quality. The sight of it seemed too much to be borne, yet she couldn't look away, fascinated as always by his splendid male beauty. It had a power and energy that only reinforced the sensation that she needed him to come fully alive.

He came back to her, looking into her slumbering gold eyes. Alex, the centre of his life. He thought how much he wanted her even when he knew she was dangerous to him. But then, didn't beauty and danger only heighten passion?

A bitter knowledge.

Whatever else happened, her body would remember him, acknowledge him master. She had walked away from him without a backward glance. Shut him out. Yet a bonfire burned inside him, stoked from the glowing embers that he could never extinguish. The scent of her was like that of some wonderful rare flower drenching the air. The scent that had always drugged him and kept him in her power.

Slowly, deliberately, he drove her crazy with his attentions, revelling in her rapid breathing, the tiny little involuntary movements of her body as he applied pressure to each sensitive spot.

"I'll die if you don't come to me," she gasped.

He didn't answer. She wouldn't die. Alex the fragile was very strong. He banked the coursing of his own wild blood though his whole body was trembling from the effort.

Abruptly she began to cry. Very softly. *Real* tears.

Why? God knows she had rejected *him*.

"Alex don't." Unable to sustain it, he tongued a glistening tear into his mouth.

"Don't deny me, Scott. I can't bear it." Her lovely mouth quivered. She sounded physically helpless.

At that, his last vestige of control snapped. Exultant, he slipped his hand beneath her spine, raising her higher, enfolding her as they began a fevered love dance, a dance that brought them perfectly together. All these weeks, months, years... Could anyone run away from their true love? No more than from their own nature.

He wanted to tell her he loved her, that without her his life was empty, songless, without joy, but his damaged pride held sway. Instead, he kissed her deeply, roughly, to a drowning ecstasy. The tumult gathered, coming for him like a great wave, ready to catch him up, sweep him along its high, foaming crest, then down into the fabled world of bliss.

There was nothing like this. *Nothing.*

"Alex," he started to murmur over and over, but her mouth rose to his, soft, tender, passionate.

"Kiss me. Kiss me," she begged frantically. "Keep kissing me." Her hair was all over her face, between them, like soft, fragrant silk. Folding him to her.

How could he refuse her? Never…never…

CHAPTER EIGHT

A RETURN polo match followed by dinner and dancing had been scheduled for the end of the month on Main Royal, keeping Wyn busy with the arrangements. Her latest book was safely with her editor, so she was able to give the planning her full attention. All the players, their wives and girlfriends were to be accommodated either at the homestead, which had twelve bedrooms, or in the bungalows. Peter had volunteered to give up his bedroom for the occasion and sleep in the bunkhouse, which worked in very well.

Valerie, as was her wont, had already advised Wyn she would be arriving a few days early. Her parents had taken off for Phuket and she was lonely. Besides, she was sure Wyn would appreciate her help with the preparations. Valerie was in her element when it came to arranging and attending polo parties. This would be in the nature of a dress rehearsal for when she was mistress of Main Royal, Wyn was given to understand. Not that Wyn needed any help. She had been doing this kind of thing for many long years. Highly successfully, too, but Valerie's manner somehow implied she had reached her use-by date. Valerie's superconfidence could do with a few grace notes, Wyn considered.

"So what are *you* going to wear, darling?" Wyn asked Alex one morning when they were discussing various dishes for the dinner menu. Succulent Main Royal beef for the main course had been decided; perhaps crab salad with noodles for the entree or some delicious Moreton Bay "bugs"—baby lobsters—served with a brandy sauce. They could have the seafood flown in.

"I haven't actually got anything," Alex answered, still leafing through a wine and food cookbook and stopping on the page featuring angel-hair pasta wrapped with Tasmanian smoked salmon.

"That's why I'm asking. You'll want something new," Wyn said fondly, "or is there something in your wardrobe you can send for?"

"Oh, I don't want to dazzle anyone, Wyn," Alex murmured in a preoccupied voice. "What about my amber silk? Everyone likes it." She passed the cookbook to Wyn, pointing to the pictured salmon dish.

"And very chic it is, too. The *dress*, not the smoked salmon. But I feel you need something new. Something really lovely to celebrate your recovery."

"I'm not fully recovered *yet*, Wyn," Alex warned.

"I mean you're responding exceptionally well to your therapy, dear."

"Yes, but I somehow feel a full recovery is a long way ahead," Alex answered a little dismally, causing Wyn to send her a searching look.

"It's not like you to be pessimistic, darling."

"I have to face up to the situation all the same, Wyn."

"But what would you do if you couldn't go back to your dancing?" Wyn asked carefully.

"Yes, tell us, Alex. I'd really like to know." Scott came up behind them with his soundless tread and stood behind Alex.

"I'll face that when the time comes."

"Maybe you should face it now." He moved to take the armchair opposite her, the very picture of the high-mettled male.

"I'll let you know as soon as I possibly can."

She answered shortly, provoked, yet she had never

looked more lovely to him, more remote. "Anyway, Peter tells me you're doing wonderfully well."

"True." Alex nodded her head, battling with the hurt that never seemed to leave her. "For normal purposes the leg is fine. The real test will come when I try to perform."

He tried to comfort her in spite of himself. "Never fear, Alex. You'll make it. After all, ballet is your *life*." Even then, the bitterness crept in.

His meaning was perfectly clear.

"Have you time for a cup of coffee, dear?" Wyn asked hastily, hoping both of them would let the matter drop.

"That'll be great!" He put his hands behind his head and sighed. "I'll have to sack Hargreave. I've given him enough chances but it's not working out. He's causing trouble among the men."

"I thought he came with a reference, dear," Wyn said with a frown.

"Maybe he wrote it himself," Alex offered with a certain dryness. She remembered Hargreave now. A powerfully built man, late thirties, good-looking in a rough way. Mean eyes.

Scott glanced over at her. "Do I look like I'd accept that? I checked with the station he worked for. They said he knew his job, but forgot to mention his abrasive nature. Money has gone missing, as well. It never did before."

"So sack him, dear," Wyn said. "Get it over with." She rose out of her chair and moved towards the door. "I'll go tell Ella to make tea and coffee. I know she baked this morning, so we're in luck."

"Where's Peter?" Scott asked when they were alone. "He's never far from your side. Unless there's a stampede." It was unworthy of him but he was getting thoroughly browned off with the young man and his desperate crush on Alex.

She brushed a lock of hair impatiently from her forehead. Scott could be downright maddening when he wanted to be. "Don't bring it up again. *Please*."

"Darling, you could have been back in hospital right now."

"I'm really getting on your nerves, aren't I?"

"Peter certainly is," Scott admitted. "Maybe I'm a bit uptight."

"You *are*." Her glance ran to the door, then back to him. She went to get up but he put out a detaining hand.

"Sorry. Sorry. Sleeping together wasn't a good idea."

"I thought it was great at the time," she returned in a rush.

He looked at her a moment, caught her upset. "Why are we doing this to each other?" His expression was serious, sombre.

"We can't help it, really."

"I suppose not. Not when we're seriously dedicated to messing up one another's lives."

"There's no one in this world I care more for."

He shook his head. "Cut the baloney, Alex. It doesn't matter. When are you going to come riding with me?"

"Any time you ask me," she said, surprised.

"You haven't seen the Blue Lady Lagoon lately. It's covered in waterlilies. Quite a sight. What about tomorrow morning before it gets too hot?"

"I'd like that." She was quiet. "We have to talk, Scott," she said finally.

"What about?" His blue-green eyes turned hostile, wary.

"You're so determined to be difficult!" She flushed, turning her head.

"Alex, what is talking going to achieve?" he asked.

"We lead different lives. Why don't you wait until you see your consultant. Once he gives you the okay, you'll be off like a shot. Back to where you belong."

"And what if he doesn't give me the okay?"

"You surely don't think I'll ask you to marry me? *Again*."

"Wouldn't you?"

He stared at her, his expression mock-incredulous. "Second best, honey. No thanks. And haven't you forgotten Valerie? I thought you were concerned about her."

"I was a little." Alex did her best to recover. "But Valerie can look after herself. She'll be here next Wednesday. Did Wyn tell you?"

"Actually no." For a moment he looked annoyed. "When did this come about?"

"Surely it's no surprise. Wyn was under the impression it had all been discussed. Ask her."

"I intend to," he said. "Of course, we both know Wyn is somehow hoping for a miracle. She just won't face the fact they don't happen."

"Oh yes, they *do*!" Alex burst out fervently. "I still believe in them."

"You surprise me, Alex," Scott drawled. "How could you possibly consider giving up your illustrious career?"

"Few dancers in my position would," she returned sharply.

"I appreciate that. Anyway, Alex, if there was ever a time I believed life with me would satisfy you, I don't now. In the end, people define themselves by their actions. You're a dancer. You have your career. My passion is Main Royal."

They rode out as the dawn wind was chasing the last sprinkling of stars from the sky. Alex, on this morning of mornings, felt she had no right to the happiness that welled within her. Even Scott looked at peace, his handsome face free of all tension. He was as much at ease with the magical morning as she was, both of them drawing in the marvellous scents of the bush—the vapour of eucalypts drawn off by the rising sun; the sweet, penetrating fragrance of boronia, lilies, wild fruits and berries. Even the grasses smelled sweet, the wind caressing their waving tops and shaking out the freshness.

As the bush came alive, the sun rose, climbing into a sky that was bluer, clearer, higher than anywhere else on earth. Birdsong floated for miles over the great mulga plains, swelling over the desert where the dunes were turning a fiery red.

Off in the distance against a tapestry of flowering bauhinias, a herd of animals grazed belly-deep—kangaroos, the big reds, smaller tans, blues and greys alongside the high-stepping flightless emus that stood taller than she did. Even as Alex looked, a pair of young kangaroo broke away from the pack, shadow-boxing on their hind legs. How often she had seen it. Always entertained.

When she had first arrived on Main Royal, Scott had brought her an adorable little joey to look after. It had lost its mother and he had asked her to feed it, to love it, to see it didn't die. Even when it grew into a big red and returned to the wild, it often came back to the main compound to say hello, following Alex around much as any domestic pet would have done. It had still been coming in when she left. Her own faithful Robby. Wyn had told her Robby hadn't been seen for some time. Probably it had mated, had a family, gone off to the distant hills. She cherished the memory of the gentle little creature it had been; the way looking after it had quietened her own grief. Scott was in everything good that had happened to her.

She sat easily, gracefully, in the saddle, an accomplished rider who could interpret every passing whim and tension in the fine horses she had been privileged to ride. No quiet old workhorse for Alex. Scott had always seen to it she was properly mounted. This morning she was riding four-year-old Regina turned out to perfection. Regina was a bright chestnut with shimmering velvet eyes and muscles that rippled from shoulder to haunch, promising instant acceleration. A spirited horse with a sweet temper. Scott knew just what she liked.

Her leg was giving her no trouble at all, but she kept a firm hold on the reins. Scott rode close beside her, making sure there wasn't the slightest risk. Sometimes he moved ahead, lifting branches bearing down on them through the screen of trees. Once he pointed off to the north-west boundary where a herd of clean skins was being driven in from a muster. A cloud of red dust floated above them, the lowing like distant thunder.

Approaching the Blue Lady Lagoon, they passed through a spirit place where dozens of oddly shaped stones painted white, black, bright ochres and burnt sienna had been arranged in a series of ever-widening circles. The circle of life. Both of them spontaneously directed the horses farther up the gully so they wouldn't disturb the area. Native symbolism was important as was their rich spiritual life.

All at once into the acacia-shrouded corridor that ran along the upper reaches of the lagoon, came several clear notes—sweet, mellow, unbelievably beautiful. The limpid notes came again. Closer, more intense this time.

"Over there," Scott said in a vibrant undertone, pointing.

She only saw the tip of a feathered tail before the

bellbird disappeared into the thick undergrowth with a swish of twigs and leaves.

"Surely that's a miracle!" Alex breathed, her face radiant with delight. "Could it possibly be *our* bell-bird?"

"It might help to think so." His smile was indulgent. "We'll leave the horses here and go the rest of the way on foot." He dismounted, turned to help her, then tied the reins of both horses to a low branch.

The broad expanse of water, almost a perfect half-moon, was a rare sight. On the dark emerald water, silver-splatted by the sun, great swaths of lotus lilies held their violet heads above their broad, glossy pads. The shining waters supported beautiful reeds and wild iris, with a white-boled ghost gum standing like a totem at the far reaches of the lake.

Scott went ahead, holding out his hand in case she stumbled on one of the polished river pebbles half-embedded in the sweeping slope.

"How beautiful!" Alex exclaimed.

"We've been lucky. Winter rains. The long-term forecast is for a cyclone in the Far North late December. If that happens, we'll get the floodwaters down here."

"And the wildflowers. I'll miss out."

"Never mind. You'll have great sheaves of bouquets enclosed in cellophane instead," he answered with some irony.

"Maybe." Alex looked away, her voice barely audible. "You don't mean to marry Valerie, do you?" She was astonished she had said it. It simply popped out.

He tilted his akubra farther down over his eyes. "I want a wife, Alex. Children. I haven't enjoyed what life has been on my own." A sound distracted him and he broke off, turning in time to see a brolga land at the edge of the lagoon before beginning to practise its steps for the mating ritual. "See what I mean? We all need a mate."

"But *Valerie*?" Alex couldn't keep the dismay from her voice.

"What is it? You're *jealous*?"

"I worry all the time about you," she said with perfect truth.

"No, Alex." He gave her a hard, disturbing smile. "You don't. Anyway, I don't want to talk. Let's just enjoy the peace and beauty." He took her hand and drew her down to the water's edge. "God, how I love this place."

"So do I." She lifted her head, her eyes fixed on a flight of black cockatoos with their distinctive scarlet tails. "You've no idea how much I miss it when I'm in the city."

He laughed. "But then you pick yourself up and dance, dance, dance. What are you going to do when your dancing days are over? Unless you intend to go on and on like Fonteyn."

"Not many do that." She shook her head. "Neither do they rise to her eminence. I suppose, providing I'm *able* to return, I might last into my late thirties."

"The right time for having children will almost be past."

"I know."

"Don't you *care*?"

"Good heavens, yes, Scott. Sometimes I'm afraid I'll be left all alone again like I was when my parents were killed."

"You had Wyn. You had me."

"I don't think I would have survived without you," she said emotionally, her fingers twisting in his.

"Maybe not so well, but you'd have survived. There's

something quite remarkable about you, Alex. In some ways you're tougher than I am."

"How could that ever be? You couldn't point to a single instance."

"Men mightn't shed easy tears, Alex, but they know how to bleed. Women are supposed to be the romantic ones, but men have their dreams, too. Terrible things can happen when they're dashed. Unlike me, you reject our shared memories. There was a time when you held me in the palm of your hand. From a long, wonderful, pure relationship, we became lovers. Thinking back, you know, I can almost laugh."

"I was a virgin, Scott," she broke in.

"I know. There was no one else in your life but me. Only when it was time to make it official, you called the whole thing off."

"That's not what I did and you know it."

"Oh yes, you did, my darling. How many men have you been to bed with since?"

"Including you?" she retorted fiercely, responding to the cool insolence of his tone. "To use your own words, Scott, it's none of your business."

"When I regard you as family?" His aqua eyes glittered with mockery.

"We had such a beautiful relationship when I was a child," she sighed.

"Didn't we? Now we don't get on at all. Fatal attraction might explain it. Maybe that's all we had of value in the first place."

She stared at him, wanting to hit him. "I won't let you say that. We share a bond."

"You don't consider it ruptured?"

"Neither do you from your behaviour."

"You mean making love to you?" He spoke sardonically.

"*I* wanted it just as much as you. I mean putting yourself at risk for me, Scott. Occasionally we even slide back into our old ways. When we first rode out, you looked utterly at peace."

"Darling, I *was*. I was daydreaming our separation had never been. You know how much I want you, Alex, but it only makes me angry inside. I'm not ever really going to be free of you but I have to get on with my life. You do see that, don't you? You'll resume your climb to the very top. You may well go to London and join the Royal Ballet as some of your predecessors have done. There's no telling where your career might take you."

"You're very sure I'm going to make a complete recovery." Her eyes rose to his, golden, poignant.

"I've never seen anyone more motivated in my life."

She turned her head away to conceal her grief. No matter what she said or what happened to her in the future, he would never forgive her for what he saw as her betrayal. "Shall we ride on?" she suggested, keeping the pain from her voice.

"Only if you want to." There was a lot of emotion in him, as well.

"Scott?"

He shook his head.

"I love you. I'll *always* love you. Please believe it."

"No."

To her anguish he seemed to recoil. Abruptly, tears welled into her eyes. Had she imagined for one moment she could regain his trust? Twice in his life, Scott had been left by a woman he loved. His mother and her. No one knew better than Alex how totally unsuccessful Stephanie had been in her efforts to re-establish a close bond with her son. It was impossible to breach the walls.

Forgetting her knee, acting on impulse, Alex began to run.

Run.

There was no discomfort. She was covering the ground like a gazelle, only in her haste she failed to see the hump of a large river rock all but hidden in the sand. She staggered, almost fell, quickly regained her balance as Scott closed in on her, grasping her strongly around the waist.

"For God's sake, what are you trying to do?"

"Get away from you." She was fast losing her self-control. "Damn you, Scott. *Damn you.* You and your insufferable pride. You're not human at all."

"Aren't I?"

Though she was struggling madly, he spun her around to him with the passionate impetus of any of her partners, holding her ruthlessly while his mouth bore down on hers, found it.

For a moment, his mind reeled as memories came rushing back to him, memories retained forever in dreams. Alex was the source of all pleasure and pain. She wouldn't relinquish her hold.

Though neither of them could recall afterwards precisely how they got there, they were lying in a warm sandy hollow overhung by melaleucas and ringed with a host of white Day lilies. This time, Alex helped him. Both of them moved feverishly to peel off their clothes and expose their bodies to the sun spangled air. There might have been a thousand reasons why they shouldn't make love, but the order of passion between them was a little like being out of one's mind.

When ultimately he was inside her, Alex opened her eyes. The sky was a wonderful deep blue, blindingly bright. Its brilliance seemed to increase, become a shining focus for her enraptured eyes. She was happy. *Glo-*

riously happy as her love found expression. Every little thing he did to her brought her to a point of desperate arousal. Now the ripples were beginning deep in her body, heralding the moment of climax. A moment before she came, she cried out, not bothered that anyone would hear her. Making love by their secret lagoon—this was *ecstasy*. She only truly knew who she *was* with Scott. Light-years away from the glittering theatre. And *glad* to be.

As Alex was consumed, Scott reached his own shattering point of release. There was no sense of loss, of suffering, the cold breath of loneliness. It was just as it had been when they were together. A wild and passionate splendour. He had never given himself to another woman in such a way, so completely, unconditionally, nothing held back. Alex herself was the enormous paradox, matching him in everything he did, yet capable afterwards of tearing herself from him.

It was true a woman could steal a man's heart away. And never give it back.

The freight plane arrived, bringing not only household and station supplies but a sack of mail for Alex, as well. It had been kept, then sent on to her by the Company.

Abe carried the sack up the front steps, pretending to groan under its weight. "Would a famous ballerina, Alexandra Ashton be livin' here?" he asked in an indulgent tone.

"What's this, Abe?" Alex, who had been enjoying morning tea with Wyn and Peter, sprang up to greet him.

"Fan mail, Princess. I'd say folks have been missin' you."

"Good Lord, Alex. They have indeed." Wyn looked on. "You'll have your work cut out trying to answer that load."

"That's where you come in, Wyn," Alex teased.

"Where would you like it?" Abe asked.

"I'll take care of it, Abe, if you like," Peter offered, unfolding his arms.

"Yes, leave it, Abe." Wyn was visibly considering the right place to put it.

"You're the boss!" Abe tipped a hand to his battered black akubra. He went to walk down the steps, then swung back as if he had forgotten something. "By the way, there's more liniment for you, Princess." He fished deep in his pocket, then withdrew a tall glass phial filled with a golden green viscous liquid.

"Oh, thank you, Abe. We've almost run out." Alex took the phial, tilting it so she could admire the colour of the oil in the sun. "It really is helping."

Abe nodded solemnly. "A tried-and-true remedy used by my people over a long, long time."

"You won't tell me what it is, Abe?" Peter came closer to examine the liniment as Alex passed it to him.

"Do you believe in its magic?"

"Of course he does," Alex said quickly. "He's been able to witness its efficacy first-hand."

"That is what I like to hear," Abe declared. "But it's only for *you*, Princess."

"Thank you, Abe," Alex called.

"Remember, it's precious."

"I will."

"You don't really believe this oil is extra special, do you, Alex?" Peter asked after Abe drove off.

"Why not?"

"I know you told Abe I did, but while it's certainly doing no harm, I can't say with any certainty it's all that beneficial."

Alex's eyes drifted over to Wyn's. "You really should take time to study native remedies while you're here,

Peter. Our aboriginal people have been in this country for at least one hundred thousand years. Double what was once thought. In fact, the whole question of their antiquity has to be rethought since the recent discovery and dating of the rock paintings in the Northern Territory. Is it any wonder, then, that they have an astounding knowledge of the environment and how to control illness by way of natural remedies?"

Peter made a little conciliatory sound in his throat. "I do appreciate that, Alex. Don't get me wrong. We all know about the wonderful medicinal properties of trees and plants. We depend on them for drugs. But when you get into the area of the supernatural almost..."

"Careful what you say, Peter," Alex warned. "Abe is an expert in sorcery."

"You're having me on," Peter said, laughing, managing to look a little disconcerted at the same time.

"He's a native doctor, too. I was trying to protect you when I said you believe. But Abe *knew*."

For an instant, Peter looked flabbergasted. "He's not going to hold it against me, surely?"

"No." Alex turned her head and winked at Wyn. "He's not going to give you the recipe for the liniment, either."

"Gee, I never meant to offend him." Peter looked disgusted with himself.

"Don't worry," Alex soothed. "Abe only deals in *beneficial* magic...now."

"What the heck does that mean?" Peter's eyebrows shot up.

"We think he was a kurdaitcha man at one time," Wyn answered thoughtfully, pouring herself another cup of tea. "Certainly his small toes are dislocated, which they have to be to wear the special kurdaitcha shoes. My brother, Scott's father, was convinced of it. Thirty years ago, there was some trouble in the Western desert. Injuries were done to certain members of the tribe, sacred laws were infringed, an elder was speared to death, bringing it all to a head. Tribal law had to be applied for order to be restored. It's highly likely Abe handled matters both on his own as a kurdaitcha man as well as leading the revenge expedition. All we knew was that it was all settled at a time when Abe was supposedly on walkabout."

Peter stared at her. "Good grief! I have to say he's a fairly imposing old guy."

"The singing is certainly a magical operation," Alex added with a gleam of mischief in her eyes.

"Singing? What singing?" Peter sat down again.

"It's a form of sorcery," Alex explained. "A victim is sung to death. It's not unheard of even now. Victims of a singing sicken and die. Then there's pointing the stick, or image sorcery, where a representation of the victim is painted on a rock wall."

"You won't catch me questioning one of Abe's potions again," Peter said. "Actually, now that I come to think about it, the liniment is excellent."

"It really is." Alex smiled.

The sack of mail was finally deposited in a corner of a large, beautifully furnished room, which looked out onto a horseshoe-shaped private garden with ghost gums for walls. A wonderful old structure in the classical-temple style stood in the centre, drawing the eye. The garden had been created especially for Scott's mother so she would have something beautiful to look at when she used the room as a sitting room-cum-study. Alex loved the room, too, so Wyn had it opened up for her stay.

It wasn't until late afternoon when Alex's exercise program was completed that all three of them attacked the mountain of mail—letters of support and encouragement from colleagues, friends and Alex's devoted public. Reading them gave Alex a wonderful warm feeling to know so many people cared. Tender-hearted Wyn sat with tears in her eyes, reading out extracts.

There were several packages, as well. One contained a tape from the composer, Geoffrey Simmons, who had written the score for the successful two-act ballet, *Web of Life*, created especially as a showcase for Alex. In his letter, Geoffrey explained he had included the tape of the mood music for a new ballet he and the choreographer, Gareth Williams, had begun to work on. Both of them would like feedback from Alex.

The ballet was based on an aboriginal legend about a group of beautiful young tribal women who had been turned into waterlilies for their sin of pride. Ever after, the doomed water nymphs lured young men to the lagoon to drown unless they somehow could find love and once more return to life. Geoffrey had included some sketches of proposed costumes, representing the beauty and diverse colours of one of nature's most exquisite flowers. Alex thought them gorgeous, as did Wyn.

"Let's hear the music now," Wyn suggested enthusiastically.

"If you give me a minute, I'll get my cassette player," Peter offered. Really, this was the most *fantastic* job he had ever had.

A little flair of excitement grew in Alex, too. "I'll go and get my ballet shoes. I don't know if it's the *right* moment but I'd like to dance."

"Are you sure, darling? Isn't it too soon?"

"I won't do anything foolish, Wyn. I promise."

"But you've done such a lot today. Won't you be tired?"

Alex threw up her arms. "Tired? *No*."

When she returned a short time later, she was wearing

a pink leotard with a calf-length pink floaty skirt over it. It looked perfect. She was wearing her pointe shoes, too, Wyn noticed.

I'm scared, Wyn thought. *But Alex is a professional. She must know what she is doing.* Wyn looked towards Peter, wanting to gauge his reaction.

Far from looking concerned, Peter was gazing at Alex as though she was the most enchanting creature he had ever seen. Which she *was*, Wyn supposed. No one could have mistaken Alex for anything else but a dancer—the poise of her head, the line of her body, the lovely, flowing movements that made people turn to look at her. For a year or so after her parents had been killed, Alex had turned into a frail little girl. Ballet had made her strong. And I had insisted on it, Wyn thought. Ballet had also lost Alex Scott. But Wyn couldn't dwell on that. It was all too upsetting.

Alex heard the tape through before she asked Peter to replay it. It wasn't easy music with a clear melodic line but it was wonderfully atmospheric. Alex was so familiar with lagoons and the magnificent species of wildflowers that abounded that she had no difficulty whatever getting a sense of place. The piano music spilled hauntingly into the room before Alex moved away from the open French doors and began to dance…slowly, gently, like a flower moving in the breeze.…

That was how it seemed to Scott as he paused at the open doorway. Wyn and Peter looked up, but he signalled with a movement of his hand for them to remain quiet. Noiselessly he took up a position inside the room, flattening his tall, lean body against the wall. Alex was oblivious to him. Off in her own world. Her beautiful hair was tied back with a ribbon the same pink as her costume, although the skirt was only a layer of chiffon.

He could clearly see her gleaming, slender legs. For a moment he knew Wyn's terror. Was Alex ready for this? His glittering eyes flicked towards Peter's face, but there was no worry there, just that infuriating open-mouthed look of adoration.

The music was beautiful, unusual. He couldn't pick up a clear recurring theme. It was more an evocation. It reminded him somehow of the secret haunts where he and Alex had made love. There was fantasy in it, the sound of lapping water, of bird calls, of the wind shaking out the trees. He felt so many mixed emotions as he watched her. Anguish, exhilaration, the same sense of enchantment that was holding Peter spellbound. She was so *good*, so natural, making such difficult movements look so easy.

He realised with a deep pang that he was so damned proud of her. It made him feel odd, as though he suddenly recognised he had no right whatever to the bitterness and anger that continued to plague him. Alex wasn't an ordinary young woman. She was an inspiration. He couldn't cage her any more than he could cage some wondrous bird. She had so much to offer, yet he had sought to keep her for himself.

Alex, for her part, let it all flow. The music spoke to her and she listened. Nowhere in her was there pain or fear. Not even the memory of that appalling moment in *Aurora* when she knew her partner wasn't going to catch her.

A series of little movements burst from her. She was a waterlily transformed by night into a nymph. Her petals were taking form…a human body was being moulded. A body that yearned for love. Instinct told her that her own love was hovering near her, watching. She turned with a flourish, rose *en pointe*, retained it, right hand extended, left arched over her head.

Perfect! Not the slightest wobble. Emboldened with
Scott's eyes on her, she half turned, going into an arabesque in profile, slowly raising her left leg until it was
fully extended almost as high as when she had thrilled
audiences.

When she lurched, then pitched forward to the floor,
it happened so fast even Scott with his lightning reactions couldn't get to her.

"Alex!" Wyn's wail cut across the music.

She lay so still that for a moment Scott felt an answering panic.

"Alex?" Although he had to cross the room, he
reached her before Peter, who was staring down with
hollowed eyes.

"That was *my* fault," Peter muttered.

Scott ignored him, going down on his knee, his eyes
moving swiftly over Alex's trembling body.

"It's all right. *All right.* Only a stumble." Her voice
was soft, shaken.

"It wasn't a stumble at all. You damned well *fell.*"

"Well, I wouldn't have missed it for anything."

"Crazy woman!" He turned her over, slowly, gently,
staring down into her huge eyes. "Have you hurt yourself? Can you move?"

She laughed. "I don't know."

"Don't joke, Alex. We're too damned worried. Can
you sit up?"

"Here, Scott, let me," Peter tried to intervene, but
McLaren's wide back was rigid with a kind of scorn.

"Can you sit up, Alex?" he repeated.

"Sure I can. Stop looking at me like I'm a wreck."
Alex took a long, deep breath and pushed up. "A dancer
needs a lot of courage."

She thought she could hold that arabesque. Everything
felt right. It was a shock when her knee gave way.

"Oh, this is terrible!" Wyn stood wringing her hands. "You weren't ready."

"It's my fault. I should have stopped her." Peter slammed one of his fists into the other.

"*Stop* me?" Alex gave him a comforting smile. "I'm a grown woman and I've got news for you. I've taken plenty of falls."

The muscles clenched beside Scott's mouth. "Let me get you onto the sofa."

"No." Her voice was oddly lacking in self-concern. "I'll just wait until the little cramp dies down."

"I'll say this for you," Scott sighed. "You never lose your spirit."

"You forget that dancers live every day of their lives with ailments and injuries. I've had cramps, strains, sprains. The lot."

"Why would you want to put up with anything so gruelling?" Scott asked in some exasperation.

"I'm beginning to wonder, too. I must be getting old."

"Twenty-four?" Peter felt horribly guilty. Yet again. "Alex, you'll have to put something warm over your legs," he advised.

Scott got an arm under Alex, lifted her like a feather and deposited her on the sofa.

"You would have made a great partner," Alex joked.

He didn't smile. "Cut it out."

Peter made his examination. "Nothing so far as I can see, Alex, praise the Lord! I think it was simply a case of too much too soon."

"Are you going to listen, Alex?"

Although Scott spoke sternly, Alex knew his concern.

"Foot out straight, Alex. Point your toes," Peter ordered.

"No problem, Peter. Honestly! The knee needs more work, but I know it's getting stronger."

And then you'll go away.

Scott stood motionless, staring down at her. The red-gold of the sunset was falling through the high arched windows, moving across the room until it caught fire in Alex's hair.

The sight pierced him like a stab wound.

When Wyn opened her own mail, she found a letter from Stephanie asking if she could visit Main Royal and bring a friend. It was the sort of thing Stephanie did, appealing to Wyn. Wyn had long since become the intermediary between mother and son although Scott refused his mother nothing. *Except* his old devotion. Nevertheless, Wyn had always had a certain sympathy for Stephanie.

At the time of her marriage, Stephanie had been a beautiful social butterfly. She should have remained in her environment, Wyn had thought even then. She was like a hothouse flower exposed to the elements. Station life had never appealed to her, yet she'd stuck it out as best she could until her husband's death. Then it had become intolerable.

Undoubtedly Stephanie loved her son. Indeed, she was very proud of him, but satisfying her own needs had always been very important to her. Then again, she lacked the authentic maternal streak that made countless women all over the world make any sacrifice for their children.

All the same, Wyn couldn't help liking her. Self-centred she might be, but there was no malice in Stephanie. In her mid-fifties, she was still a remarkably beautiful woman. Unfair or not, physical beauty always gave man or woman a distinct advantage.

Stephanie might as well come at the weekend when

the homestead would be full of guests. Stephanie loved people and parties. Wyn wondered who the friend might be. Stephanie's second marriage had ended in divorce but she always had some suitable admirer to hand. She would put through a call later that evening after she'd spoken to Scott. Wyn thought Stephanie would do better to speak to her son directly, but Stephanie always chose this roundabout way. At least she and Alex got on well. Stephanie had sent flowers several times to the hospital and Alex had rung her afterwards to acknowledge them. Stephanie now lived in Melbourne as she had when she was young. She and Charles had been married from Stephanie's parents' Toorak mansion.

When Wyn approached the subject after dinner, Scott responded in the same old way, eyes cool and dispassionate.

"My mother is welcome any time she cares to come, Wyn. You know that. All it takes is a phone call. If it can't be to myself, she always has you to appeal to."

"She wants to bring a friend, dear."

"Some man, I'll bet!" Scott lifted his head.

"She's very beautiful," Alex said, smiling at her old images. Stephanie dancing at balls.

"And terribly rich. And getting *richer*," Scott said.

"You've managed your mother's affairs extremely well, darling," Wyn said, kissing her nephew lightly on the cheek before making her phone call. "I know she's very grateful."

CHAPTER NINE

As SOON as Valerie saw Scott and Alex together, she had the powerful intuition something had happened. If anything, there was an increase in the peculiar tension that seemed to flow between the two of them, but Valerie was convinced there was considerable ambivalence in the relationship—a kind of irreconcilable love-hate. All through the afternoon of her arrival and the evening, anger bubbled away in Valerie until by the next morning she resolved to let Alex know it was time to get her act together and go back to Sydney. So far as Valerie was concerned, she could *keep* on going. Moscow might be a safe place.

Alex was in the midst of her water therapy when Valerie made her way through the garden to the pool area, a bright floral shirt over a very small pink bikini.

"Boy, that outfit packs quite a punch!" Peter murmured to Alex as they both turned their heads. "If it's all right with you, Alex, I think I'll take a hike. I've had about as much as I can take of Valerie's snob treatment. She thinks she's mistress of Main Royal already."

Alex looked at him apologetically. "That's okay, Peter. I'm sorry about Valerie. You deserve some time to yourself anyway."

"I thought I might do a bit of riding if young Gabe can find me a nice quiet horse."

"Oh, he will," Alex promised. "Where will you go? You can't just head off."

"Not far, Alex," Peter answered casually, squinting

his eyes against the bright glitter off the water. "I won't be gone long."

"Stick to the recognised trails," Alex advised, pulling herself out of the pool, "and don't go anywhere near Myndi Swamp. It's too heavy there for horses. If you wait a while, I'll come with you."

Peter threw a half glance in Valerie's direction. "Actually I think dear Valerie is longing to have a chat with you. Don't worry, Alex. I know how to take care of myself."

"I still want to know where you're heading, Peter," Alex said a little anxiously.

"What about Devil Hill?" Peter grinned. His tone was one of gentle ridicule.

"Peter, it's *haunted*," Alex said. "No joke. Even Abe won't go near the place. A lot of people have got into major difficulties getting too near. A McLaren relative out from Scotland disappeared and was never seen again."

"Sure I've heard that story," Peter returned, smiling calmly, "but it was nearly a hundred years ago. Probably he met up with one of your kurdaitcha men."

"Don't ignore the warning, Peter." Alex's eyes were very serious. "There are a lot of things out here that can't be explained."

Peter shrugged and gave another little smile. "I'm sorry, Alex. I know you care about me. I'll stick to the beaten track." Beautiful and sweet as she was, Alex was extraordinarily superstitious, he thought. The stories surrounding Devil Hill were fascinating, but nonsense, as well. He didn't believe in all that junk but he could see it had a lot to do with the powerful influence of a primeval land.

As they passed one another, Valerie and Peter exchanged a few words, then Valerie continued on to the pool's edge and stared down into the crystal turquoise water. There was a wonderful mosaic on the bottom of the pool that appealed to her greatly. She remembered the summer the new pool had been set in. Scott had perfect taste in everything.

"Lovely day!" Alex stood by a recliner, towelling her hair.

"Perfect as always. I don't much like that Peter," Valerie tossed over her shoulder.

For a moment, Alex couldn't trust her voice. "Valerie, you haven't come down here to be disagreeable, have you?"

"You bet," Valerie answered in a crisp voice. "So don't let's waste any more time. I make no apologies, Alex. How could you *do* it?"

"Come again?" Alex stared back at her, her topaz eyes catching fire.

"You've been sleeping with Scott," Valerie accused. "I see how you are together," she added, glaring.

Resolutely Alex began to gather her things. "Have you ever wanted to be a detective? A lady private eye?"

Valerie didn't even ponder. "I've got *you* taped," she said bitterly as she took off her floral shirt and placed it over a chair. "Why can't you leave Scott alone? Steal the man I want and you'll pay."

When Peter wasn't back by four, Alex began to worry.

"I'm sure he's all right, darling," Wyn said in a comforting voice. "He had Ella make up some sandwiches and a thermos of tea. He probably had a picnic by a billabong, then a snooze. There's so much for him to see. He told me he's fascinated with the bird life. He has a good camera, so he could be taking photographs."

"I don't think so, Wyn." Alex's voice was a little strained. "Peter isn't used to the bush."

"A real city slicker if ever I saw one!" Valerie looked up from her glossy magazine. "I just hope he's not going to be a bother to Scott."

"In what way?" Wyn asked.

"Well, surely, Edwina, it's Scott who would have to go after him if he got lost?" Valerie opened her eyes wide.

"It's not so terribly late." Wyn felt the first involuntary pang of anxiety. "He did say where he was going, didn't he, Alex?"

"*Not far* is what he said. He's riding Bonnie Belle so he couldn't come to much harm. He mentioned Devil Hill but that was only as a joke. I know he doesn't take our superstitions seriously."

"Why should he?" Valerie put down her magazine to look at Alex, aghast. "I don't myself."

Wyn took a deep breath, hardly listening. "He wouldn't go there?"

Valerie was now astonished. "You're not saying Devil Hill is *really* haunted, Edwina? Surely you don't believe that nonsense?"

"I believe in certain 'energies', Valerie," Wyn answered carefully. "Devil Hill has a strange history. Our aboriginal people have always believed it's a place of bad magic."

Valerie gave an incredulous laugh. "I'm talking substance, Edwina. Not all this spirit stuff."

"My instinct tells me he may have headed there," Alex said. "He promised me he would stick to the beaten track, but I saw his grin."

"Oh, Alex!" Wyn put a hand to her breast. "If you're really worried, we must get to Scott."

Valerie's face was suddenly angry. "Scott's working. He won't want to go off on a wild-goose chase."

"He won't want anyone on this property to come to any harm, either," Wyn answered in a stern, dignified voice. "I think you forget yourself, Valerie."

Instantly Valerie looked stricken. "I'm only thinking of *Scott*, Edwina. If Peter has done another fool thing, he can get himself out of it. I wouldn't be in the least surprised if he rode in any minute. Alex takes that fey sensation thing of hers too far."

"Maybe I do but I'm going after Scott, false alarm or not. We can't delay any longer."

"I'll come with you." Valerie too started up.

"I don't want you to, Valerie," Alex replied. "I can take the jeep. It's out the front."

She soon found Scott at the Five Mile. He was talking to the station vet but broke away as soon as he saw her drive into camp.

"You look like something's up." His brilliant eyes took in her expression.

She swallowed on a dry throat. "Probably nothing. Peter went out for a ride just before lunch. He said he wasn't going far but he's not back."

Scott considered. "If he keeps to the beaten track, he'll come to no harm."

"I don't think he has," Alex said.

"You're worried about him?" he asked quietly.

"Yes."

"I expect it's one of your premonitions. You've had them once or twice." In fact, Wyn had always said that Alex had the second sight.

"I don't know why I'm saying this but I think he's headed off to Devil Hill."

"Why the hell would he do that?" Scott exploded. "He knows it's off-limits."

Alex spread her hands in a sort of surrender. "Peter understands nothing about our world. He thinks heading out to Devil Hill is like taking a walk up the street. Good or bad auras attached to certain sites are beyond him. He might think it was a bit of a lark."

"Good God!" Scott groaned. "Ignorance is bliss. If he's gone that way there's no time to delay. I'll have to organise a search party."

"Let me come."

"No." Scott started to turn away. "Abe?"

"You want somethin' Boss?"

"Yeah. Come over here." Scott transferred his gaze to Alex. "Go back to the homestead, Alex. It may well be Peter will turn up, in which case send a runner. Gabe will do."

"I'm sorry, Scott."

Abe ambled over to them, his black liquid eyes going from one to the other. "Do we have a problem?" he asked.

"Might," Scott retorted briskly.

"Peter went off for a ride around lunchtime. He hasn't come back," Alex explained.

"So?" Abe cocked his snow-white head.

"I just have this funny feeling he's gone to Devil Hill."

"What!" Abe's expression totally changed. "You *let* him?"

"I told him not to go there, Abe," Alex defended herself. "I told him to stick to the beaten track."

"It seems likely he didn't." There was a faint impatience in Scott's voice.

Abe was silent a moment. "He laughs but the Hill has

been drawin' him all the same. Do we go in search, Boss?''

Scott nodded. "It's more or less forced on us, Abe. It'll be dark soon. And *cold*. Our visitors don't seem to realise the desert may be hot by day but it can get as cold as the stars by night.''

"I wish you'd let me come with you," Alex said again.

Both men looked past her. "Go back now, Alex," Scott said finally. "We'll take the jeep. You take my horse. Dave can go back with you for company." Scott lifted a hand, gestured to one of the men. "Dave, I'd like you to ride back with Miss Alex.''

"Sure, Boss." Dave tipped his hat. "Now?''

"Right now," Scott said and opened the door of the jeep for Alex to descend. "We might get stuck out there, Alex. It depends. Don't get into any panic. Peter's probably lost his bearings. If we're heading the right way, we'll find him fast.''

Right at dusk, Bonnie Belle came in. Riderless. Causing considerable anxiety to Alex and Wyn. Valerie, however, took it in her stride. "Probably threw him," she said with a shrug.

"Bonnie wouldn't throw anyone." Alex's lips tightened. "Aren't you the least bit concerned?''

"The only person I'm concerned about is Scott.''

"I'm sure there's no need to be," Wyn said. "Scott knows every part of the station like the back of his hand. Besides, he's got Abe with him. I don't think you could get a better duo.''

"And what if Peter has taken a fall? What if he's tried to climb the Hill and fallen into a crevice? Abe is old now. If there's any rescuing to be done, Scott will have to do it.''

Wyn leaned back in her high carved chair, regarding her. "Scott is superbly fit, dear, and he's a very experienced bushman. Our concern is for Peter. He's the only one likely to put himself in any danger.''

Valerie shook her head but remained quiet. After dinner she retired to her room, saying she had a bad headache, which seemed to be perfectly true. Alex and Wyn continued to sit up, hoping every minute they would hear the jeep sweep into the circular driveway.

Finally after midnight, Alex rose and touched Wyn on the shoulder. "I don't like to disturb you, Wyn, but I think you should go to bed. You look so uncomfortable there.''

Wyn squared her shoulders. "I'm all right, darling.''

"No, Wyn. Please go off now. You look tired.''

"But what are you going to do?''

"I'll curl up here on the sofa. I couldn't really sleep anyway. Obviously something has gone wrong.''

"I'm afraid so, my darling.'' Wyn reached out and the two women locked hands.

In the early dawn, Alex came awake instantly as she caught the distant sound of an engine. She threw off the mohair rug and made a rush for the front door, crying out Wyn's name though it was unlikely Wyn would hear her. On the veranda she searched the landscape with her eyes. The lemon streaks across the sky were being replaced by violet and rose as the sun started to climb and birds began their morning symphony.

"What is it, dear? What's up?'' Wyn in a dressing gown, her thick hair tousled from sleep, was standing in the hallway, Valerie behind her, busy tying the belt of her robe. Both women looked a little dazed.

"It's the jeep. Can't you hear it?"

Wyn touched her forehead, came out onto the veranda. "Yes, I can. Thank God."

Valerie joined them, very pale and quiet, not nearly so striking with her face devoid of make-up. Long minutes later, they heard the jeep entering the main compound. It seemed to stop for a time before proceeding on its way, the roar of the engine unnaturally loud on the still air.

As it entered the driveway, Alex expelled a long, shuddering breath. "Where's Scott?" There was no sign of him.

Valerie swept past her, going to the balustrade and leaning forward. "Yes, where is he?" she cried sharply. "That's Abe at the wheel and your Peter is in the back. He's wearing Scott's jacket."

Alex moved closer to the balustrade, as well, feeling a hollowness in her stomach. "Let's wait and see."

At her perceived calmness, Valerie's emotions seemed to skyrocket. She turned swiftly, made a grab at Alex's shoulder. "This is all your fault!" she cried, giving Alex a shove that sent her crashing into the glass-topped white wicker table.

The blood drained from Wyn's face. "Valerie," she moaned.

Valerie was past hearing. As the jeep came to a halt, she flew down the steps, demanding of Abe where Scott was, ignoring Abe's passenger.

"Are you all right, Alex?" Wyn went immediately to her goddaughter, struggling for control.

Alex nodded though she felt sick and shaken.

"But she must have hurt you."

"Forget it, Wyn. I have." Gingerly, Alex straightened up. She'd have a nice bruise on her hip.

"I won't dear." Wyn's voice was very quiet and stern. "I won't *have* it, either. Who does Valerie think she is?"

"Mrs Scott McLaren, obviously."

Valerie was still haranguing Abe when the two of them joined her on the driveway. Peter, looking very white and drawn, waved a hand. "Sorry, ladies, I've been a monumental fool."

"Broke a leg," Abe explained. "The Boss will be here soon. He's pickin' up Mrs McGuire. Her nursing training sure comes in handy."

"Why didn't you tell me that?" Valerie demanded furiously.

"Didn't give me a chance, Miss Freeman," Abe answered quietly.

"Scott's all right, isn't he, Abe?" Wyn stood with her hands clasped. It seemed to her that both men were extremely subdued.

"Sure he is, Miss Edwina," Abe reassured her. "He's got a bit of a gash on his arm that might need a few stitches. Nothin' to worry about."

"There, what did I tell you?" Valerie's voice came hard and accusing.

Alex didn't answer. She looked towards the entrance, the whitewashed stone walls smothered in great bracts of scarlet bougainvillea. Scott, looking as vital as ever, walked through with a tall, middle-aged woman—Mary McGuire, the wife of Scott's overseer. Mary had had many years of experience with the Flying Doctor Service before retiring to live full-time on the station with her husband.

As soon as Valerie saw Scott, she did a mad about-face, turning and running into the house. She wanted to get herself together. She wasn't wearing make-up and not looking her best.

As they got closer, it became apparent that Scott had been injured. There was blood all over the left sleeve and the front of his shirt.

Little tremors ran through Alex's body. She flew towards him, crying out his name.

He put out an arm and gathered her in. "You know Peter has broken a leg?"

"What happened to *you*?" she demanded. Poor Peter would have to wait.

He quirked an eyebrow, his gaze faintly quizzical. "Nothing life threatening. Hey, what's the matter? I'm fine."

"It looks worse than it is, Alex," Mary McGuire interjected, trying to offer reassurance, a little alarmed at Alex's pallor. "Here, Scott," she said sharply. "I think she's going to faint."

"I'm not!" Even so, the immediate world was a blur.

Somehow she was sitting on the side of the three-tiered stone fountain, Scott's hand holding her head down. She tried to speak. Could not. It was moments before her head rose.

"She didn't go to bed at all," Wyn was saying. "She slept on the sofa."

"Maybe some strong, sweet tea," Mary suggested. "I'll go see to the young man. Scott has given him pain-killers, but he'll need more." Mary moved off.

"Feeling better now, Alex?" Scott asked, his brilliant eyes searching her face.

"Yes. Thank you." She shook her bright head as if to clear it.

"Since when did you faint at the sight of blood?" he asked in an impossibly tender voice.

"Since today. I didn't actually faint."

"You came damn near it. What happened to Valerie? I saw her take off like a rocket."

"I imagine she's making herself beautiful for you," she told him wryly.

Scott was silent for a time. "I'll have to confront this, won't I?"

"*This*?" She lifted her head.

"This...*situation*. It's gone on long enough."

Midmorning, the Flying Doctor flew in and transferred Peter to Longreach Base Hospital. The break wasn't bad, but the leg had to be set in plaster; Peter also seemed to be in a severe state of shock. Admittedly doped up, he had told them a long, garbled story about voices calling to him at Devil Hill; of shadowy figures, spine-chilling noises. Although he insisted he'd had no intention of visiting the place, some force outside himself had drawn him to the site, relic of an extinct volcano from a past geological age. Unlike the other great rocks of the Interior—the giant tors, the monoliths, ranges and spurs—Devil Hill never went through fantastic colour changes. It remained from sun-up to sundown a peculiar greyish black. Climbing the eastern slope where the rock face was less jagged, Peter had suddenly, inexplicably, lost his footing and rolled into a deep crevice without vegetation except for some repulsive fungilike growths.

"God, I was scared," he told them and gave Alex a weak smile. "You did warn me, Alex."

"I did indeed."

"Never mind, Peter," Scott consoled. "It'll make a good after-dinner story."

Only Valerie laughed in a hollow, sarcastic way. "And a tall one, too."

Scott gazed across at her, a strange light in his eyes. "You wouldn't say that if you'd been with us last night, Val. There's some *presence* there, I swear it."

Valerie stared back at him dumbly. "You're surely not serious?"

"I'm not going to pretend anything, Val. So far as I'm concerned, we were lucky we got off with a broken leg and a gash. I don't know if I could have found Peter so quickly, either, except for Abe. He seemed to guide me by instinct. Abe's no ordinary man."

"Neither are you." Valerie sounded affronted on his behalf.

Scott shook his head. "I've lived here my whole life. My family pioneered this station, but I'll never know what Abe knows. He's one with this ancient land. He sees its mysteries. All the time we spent on the Hill, he never stopped chanting, one intonation after the other, warding off the bad spirits."

"So that's why the both of you wouldn't take me," Alex said quietly.

Scott nodded. "No question. Unfortunately this brings Peter's stay with us to an end. He knows that himself. When he's feeling fit enough to travel, I'll have him flown home. He has his family and his girlfriend."

"That's if his girlfriend is still around." Valerie laughed. "I suppose at your first appearance back on stage you'll see him sitting up in the front row, Alex." She laughed again.

Alex simply ignored that. "Poor Peter!" she sighed. "It's a pity it had to end this way. He was having such a good time and he was a tremendous help to me."

Scott stood up, patted her shoulder. "Don't worry, Alex," he said dryly, "he'll make a speedy recovery."

Later in the day, Alex was going half-heartedly through her barre exercises when Scott walked into the room, a glitter to his expression, the very picture of restless energy.

The prowling panther, Alex thought. She couldn't explain the complexity of her passion for him.

She stopped her gentle battements, her eyes questioning. "How's the arm now?" He looked a little pale beneath his bronze tan.

"Giving me a bit of gyp." He put his hand into his armpit, easing the shoulder. "I've got so many things to do, but I'm on edge."

"I can see that," she returned gently. "It won't hurt to take some time off. That can't have been a pleasant experience last night."

He looked at her, shook his head wonderingly. "It was downright nerve-racking. God knows what's buried under that hill."

Alex crossed to a chair, picked up a soft towel and began patting the beads of perspiration from her temples. "It would take an awful lot to scare you."

"I like to know what I'm confronting, thank you, ma'am. Anyway, we won't worry about that. I've been talking to Wyn."

"Oh?" She feigned ignorance even though she had a good idea what the talk was about.

"She told me Valerie all but attacked you."

"I suppose she did." Alex continued to speak mildly.

"You seem to be taking it very lightly."

She turned to face him, skin glowing from her exertions. "What do you want me to do, Scott? Isn't Valerie your good friend?'' She knew her tone held an infuriating challenge.

"You didn't say anything to provoke her?"

"*Provoke* her?'' Alex could feel herself getting angry. "I don't *care* what I said. Where does she get off thinking she can knock people around? I call that assault.''

"Of course it is,'' he agreed tersely. "I'm not condoning it in any way, Alex. I just want to know what set her off.''

"I suppose she's had enough of our *togetherness*, Scott.''

His glittering eyes narrowed. "What would she know about it?''

"She's had a damn good guess.''

"So she thought she could knock you over?''

"To put it plainly, I think she would have liked to have done more than that.''

"Dear God.'' Scott looked past her tawny head to the open windows. "I have to say I'm appalled.''

"Really?'' Alex's topaz eyes sparkled. "Didn't you realise your Val is exceptionally high-handed, not to say arrogant. I'd hate to have to work for her.''

"And you did nothing? You, who can go off like a firecracker?''

"Only with *you*,'' Alex said shortly. "I don't go around attacking people. I don't believe in it.'' She realised with a shock there were tears in her eyes. She was pretty tired. It had been a stressful night and the morning hadn't been much better.

"I certainly don't intend to let the incident pass,'' Scott said.

"I was afraid you wouldn't.''

"Oh, *Alex*!'' he groaned softly and pulled her to his side.

"I'm tired." She rested gracefully, pliantly, against him, her forehead pressed into his uninjured arm.

"Why are you working away here?" he asked. "You had a bad night." As he spoke, he was studying their reflections in the mirrored wall behind the barre. She was so flowerlike, the line of her body so fluid, so silken and serene, like the stem of a tulip. Tall, dark-skinned, he thought he looked like a wild frontiers man beside her. His hair needed cutting. It was curling into his neck.

"I have to keep going, Scott. Practise every day," she was saying.

"What if the knee doesn't hold up?"

"I'll settle for *you*," she murmured with the hint of a smile.

"Will you?" His voice was deeply sardonic. "I don't believe I asked."

"And I understand that perfectly." She lifted her head, her huge eyes glistening, and as she did so his arm clutched convulsively around her slender body.

"It will never be over between us, will it?"

"You wish it were?"

"Not this minute." His hand slid down to shape her nape. "All I want right now is to kiss you. You're perfect to me." His fingers tugged at the ribbon that held her hair back. Released, it sprang out beneath his hand, masses and masses of Pre-Raphaelite hair.

Her mouth parted of its own accord, the tip of her tongue visible between her small white teeth. The flash of his eyes showed his answering arousal. Catching up her cushiony, soft lips, he bent his head, affected by the same powerful sensuality that affected her.

"Come to me, my love."

Valerie, searching the house for Scott, reeled in the open doorway. She knew a moment of total disorientation as if she believed this could never happen. It was a wonder she didn't scream, the sight of them together put her in such a frenzy. Scott had never kissed her like that; so passionately, so masterfully, so intimately, yet with a curious vulnerability. His hand was shaping her breast, cupping it like a perfect rose. Something inside Valerie snapped.

"I don't believe this. I *can't* believe it," she cried. "This is wrong, wrong, wrong. Stop it, Scott." She would never get the sight of them out of her mind. Both of them laying themselves wide open to the other. No holding back. That moment, Valerie abandoned all hope of ever getting Scott McLaren to commit to her. Whatever the outcome of his relationship with the hated Alexandra Ashton, he would never fight free of her spell.

Scott and Alex both turned to look at Valerie, standing so rigidly, so exposed, in the doorway, Scott predictably in control, arrogant head thrown up, his remarkable eyes sparkling with emotion. But not for her. Never for her. She wasn't so sweet. So luscious.

"I'm sorry, Val." He spoke then. "Neither of us wishes to hurt you."

"Liar!" Valerie stormed into the room, her body throbbing with outrage. "You made me believe you were through with her. That you wanted me."

"I tried to be honest with you, Val," Scott continued in the same quiet tone. "You knew what you were getting into. It seemed to work."

"Work? How could it possibly work with this creature around?" A sob rose in Valerie's throat. "I begged her not to come out here."

"I knew you visited Alex in hospital," Scott said.

"So? She had to tell you, didn't she?"

"She *didn't* tell me, Val. I checked it out. Something

you said. She didn't tell me about your attack on her this morning, either."

"Oh, Scott. Drop this, please," Alex begged, her expression pained.

"You little wimp," Valerie sneered. "You wanted to elicit some sympathy. I *had* to be the bad guy." It wasn't just jealousy burning furiously inside her. It was outraged pride.

"Wyn told me, Valerie." Scott's tone was flat. "It was Wyn who decided to speak up. Alex is family."

"*Family*." Valerie's eyes spat venom. "Forgive me if I find that funny. You think I don't know what's been going on?"

"Surely you haven't been peering through blinds?"

Alex moved to leave the room. This didn't really concern her. Scott had never loved Valerie.

Valerie extended an arm, palm up, for all the world like a policewoman on traffic duty. "Don't you *dare* leave!"

That did it. "Get out of my way, Valerie." Alex faced the other woman down.

"I want this situation resolved. *Right now*." Valerie spoke with high drama.

"Aren't you making a great deal of our affair, Val?" Scott asked. "You might put a little of the blame on yourself. But maybe women don't do that."

"So I chased you!" Valerie said with a furious laugh. "That's common knowledge. I went after you for all I was worth but I didn't know about your obsession. I'd heard about it, of course. But I had to see it for myself. No matter what she's done, you want her. She's half your size but she keeps you on a leash."

"I wish I'd thought of that!" Scott said, acidly watching Alex flee the scene. "Alex isn't entirely free of me, either. Whatever the situation, Valerie, it's *my* affair. I'm sorry for your hurt, but you don't imagine you're the only one who's ever been hurt? We all have our turn.''

Fury raged through Valerie's veins. ''I want to go home,'' she announced. ''I don't want to spend another minute here in this house. You've humiliated me, Scott, in front of all my friends. I'll be forced to miss the polo and dinner-dance. I was so looking forward to it. I have a marvellous new dress, damn you.''

''I'll fly you out whenever you're ready to go, Val,'' Scott interrupted her tirade. ''Don't feel you have to miss out on anything on my account. So far as your friends are concerned, our affair died a natural death.''

''So you'll marry her after all?'' Valerie asked, her disappointment pressing on her like a vice.

Scott's answer was a long time coming. ''There's only one thing you forgot, Valerie. It's this. Alex is already married. To her career.''

Valerie was astonished by the pain she saw there.

They were too busy on the Friday to spend much time discussing Valerie's abrupt departure. Scott had used the station helicopter to fly Valerie home and he wasn't very forthcoming when he got back. To make it worse, Jack McGuire had come up to the homestead to report that some fifteen head of cattle had been shot at Kalalah Crossing. Prime beasts, too. It was a senseless, wanton piece of butchery.

''Who would ever have done such a thing?'' Scott couldn't keep his voice from shaking with anger.

''God knows!'' Jack McGuire's face was taut with answering concern. ''Maybe some fella got drunk and went on a shooting spree. The station's so big we can't police it. Some nutter could be camping out anywhere on the property. We've had our weird characters on the station before this.''

"Post some of the men out tonight," Scott ordered. "Who needs a lunatic around the place? People will be flying in tomorrow or coming overland. They'll be everywhere. We've got the dinner-dance going at the house. I'll take the helicopter up first light. That's the only way we can cover the territory."

"Want me with you, Boss?" McGuire asked.

"No, Jack, I need you on the ground. I'll go up on my own."

Two station hands patrolled the homestead while the women stayed indoors trying to concentrate on preparations for the party. Midmorning, Scott set down on the front lawn after an unsuccessful surveillance flight.

"Nothing," he said grimly when they came out to greet him. "At least nothing I could spot. There are just so many places a man could hide. That's if he's still on the property."

"Does no one come to mind, dear?" Wyn asked worriedly. "We've had nothing like this happen before. We've had our share of cattle duffing in the past but never this senseless slaughter."

"What about that man you sacked...Hargreave?" Alex asked suddenly as the man's face swam into her mind.

"I wouldn't think he could be so vicious or so stupid," Scott considered.

"He had very mean eyes," Alex pointed out. "Whenever I saw him, I sensed a hidden cruelty."

Scott pushed to his feet. "In that case, I'll go see if Sergeant Harper can check out his whereabouts. They're sending a man in any case. Hargreave just can't vanish, though it could be we're onto the wrong man."

"You said yourself he was in an ugly mood when you fired him." Alex's instincts were working overtime. "One of the jackeroos told me he was terribly envious of you, the man who has everything. He might have thought killing some of the cattle was a way of getting even."

Scott gave a brief laugh that was boiling with fury. "If it's Hargreave, I intend to make him pay dearly."

Yet the station remained quiet. Around midafternoon Abe came up to the house to check on the household and patrolling men.

"Where's Scott now?" Alex asked, standing with Abe on the veranda. Her eyes focused on the shimmering hills. The mirage was abroad, tricking the eye. At any moment she expected to see Hargreave's head pop up from behind some shrub.

"Left him at the crossing," Abe said. "The cattle have been buried in a mass grave. The men are pretty angry, I can tell you. Reckon if it's Hargreave they'll scalp 'im."

"Do you think it could possibly be him?"

Abe frowned. "Why not? He hates the Boss. He hates him for the man *he* will never be."

Alex had gone out to the storeroom looking for various vases for the flowers that would be arranged the next morning when Wyn saw one of the patrolmen move up the steps onto the veranda. Or *was* it one of the patrolmen? Surely they weren't as tall or as thickset. She felt a little sick. The man had a rifle. A .33.

Wyn swallowed hard. She had a vague memory of the man's shape. Alerted, she struggled to shut the heavy front door but it was too late. His expression slightly crazed, the man reached her, compelling her back into the hallway.

"What is it? What do you want?" Wyn demanded, pitching her voice so one of patrolmen might hear her.

The man tilted his wide-brimmed hat back slightly. *Hargreave*. "Take it easy, lady," he said in a voice like gravel. "It's your high-and-mighty nephew I'm after." A thick purple vein beat in his forehead.

Wyn didn't even pause to consider. "How dare you come here?" she thundered. "I'll call the men."

"Could be they won't hear you." The man laughed chillingly, causing Wyn to clutch at her throat. "You surely don't mean—"

"Just a crack on the skull, lady. Don't panic. I don't hate those guys."

"But you *did* kill our cattle?"

He grinned sarcastically. "Won't say it was me, but *someone* was lookin' to give almighty McLaren a nasty surprise."

"He's been onto the police. You know that?" Wyn stared into the man's face.

"Don't care much," Hargreave said. "I know how to lose myself for a long, long time. After my little show-down with McLaren, o' course. A bit of bush justice. Can't get a job no more. You know that? McLaren puts out the word and everyone listens. So where is he? I know he's not here."

"Do you think I'd tell you even if I knew?" Wyn's chest was heaving.

"What about the little ballerina? Where's she?"

"She's with Scott," Wyn lied convincingly. "There's no one here but Ella, our housekeeper, and a couple of the house girls."

"Well, I sure don't want to converse with them,"

Hargreave sneered. His small eyes swept around. "Maybe a reward for leavin' you alone."

"If you mean money, I don't have any."

"Pull the other leg." He laughed nastily. "You McLarens are stinkin' rich."

"I mean *cash*. You've been drinking," Wyn accused. The man was slurring his words and sweating heavily.

"Doesn't matter anyway," he muttered. "I wanna find McLaren while it's still light. When them two hotheads come to, they're gonna have sore old heads, courtesy of me."

He turned, staggered a little, then went to walk back onto the veranda.

It was what Wyn *saw* that caused her to delay him with a question. "How do you possibly think you can get away with this?"

The man looked back at her almost uncomprehendingly. "What have I actually *done*, lady? Nothin' much. McLaren has everything. *Everything*. I have nothin'. Had a wife once. She ran off with another bloke. Caught up with her. Knocked her around a bit. The bloke won't be foolin' around again neither."

He lurched towards the stairs, only then catching sight of a horse and rider galloping off in the direction of the crossing.

"Ain't that the little ballerina?" he shouted. "That *hair*!"

Wyn flung the door to. Locked it. Her heart was thumping so painfully in her chest she thought it possible she might have a heart attack. Desperately she ran into the drawing room where the French doors were open. But Hargreave was already running down the front steps, rounding the house to the thicket of desert oaks where he had left his horse. He mounted it without pausing to look back at the young stockmen who were fighting to regain consciousness.

No one was gonna give McLaren any warning, he thought vengefully. And that was what that fool girl was doin'. Ridin' bareback, too. Obviously she hadn't had time to saddle up. When he got close enough, he would fire off a shot that *might* cause her to fall off. Then again, a rifle shot would alert McLaren and any of the men working close in. Hargreave licked his swollen lips and galloped after her.

Scott thought he would never forget the sight of Alex riding the black colt, Mercury, into the camp crossing. She was perched like some fairytale creature on the animal's sleek back, her full skirt hitched up, showing the full length of her beautiful straight legs. What was even more incredible, she was riding the colt without a saddle, even if mercifully she had reins.

"Alex, for the love of God!" He sprang to the colt's head, caught the reins, the power in his body visible, and grasped Alex as she slid breathlessly down Mercury's gleaming side. "Alex?" His voice cracked as she crumpled like a heartbroken doll.

"It's Hargreave," she panted, her face streaked with dust. "He's coming after you. He was at the homestead."

"But the men on patrol? *Alex*?" She slumped forward and he gathered her aching body up, his mind filled with anxiety. "Sweetheart, why the hell did you risk yourself?"

"I'm all right." She shook her head at him. "So's Wyn. He came after me. He's got a horse. He's out there somewhere. And Scott, he's got a *gun*."

"Has he, by God?" He spoke so softly, so gently, yet she shivered.

It was only when she was huddled on a blanket did Alex see Abe.

"I was coming back from the storeroom," she told them, her delicate shoulders involuntarily heaving. "I almost sang out to Wyn to let her know I'd found what we wanted, but something stopped me. I heard them talking. I rushed back outside to find Mike and Gary but both of them were out cold. When I crept back into the house, he was telling Wyn he was going after you. He wasn't threatening Wyn. It's you he wants, Scott. I grabbed Mercury off a strapper. I didn't have time to saddle up."

"You're going to be sore and sorry, Princess." Abe squeezed her hand.

"For sure." She rubbed at her leg. "What are we going to *do*, Scott? He's drunk, he's armed and he's dangerous."

He lifted her face, kissed her. "You just leave that to Abe and me. You've done more than enough."

Why not? I love you so much.

In the end, Hargreave rode right into the trap, swearing ferociously as he tried to free himself from the lasso Scott dropped on him from an overhead branch. Minutes later, stockmen converged on the spot, muttering angrily and standing over Hargreave as he sat neatly trussed on the ground. They would have to hold him overnight. Sergeant Harper would arrive in the morning and someone from the stock squad.

It took ages for the station to settle with the news flying from bungalow to bungalow and around the camp sites. It wasn't until after Hargreave had been secured in the lockup with a man posted outside his door that everyone began to quiet down. Every last man, woman and child had heard about Alex's frantic ride, most agreeing that even for an experienced horsewoman it had been some ride, all the more extraordinary because of her unique position as a dancer and the fact she was still convalescing. It seemed impossible they could face a gala day, but too late now to cry off. Any event on Main Royal was judged one of the highlights of the social calendar.

Alex spent a long time soaking in the bath, sinking into the scented water, letting the bubbles tickle her nose. Although Scott and Wyn feared the consequences of her bareback ride, apart from the soreness and the lower-back ache Abe had promised, she was happy. There had been scary moments when she thought Hargreave would fire at her. For all that, she would do it again. Nothing in the world would have mattered had anything happened to Scott. In the final analysis, only loved ones mattered. Not money. Not acclaim. It was love alone that gave meaning to life. It had taken time for her to see that. She hadn't been disappointed with her career. It had been very useful, showing her her own value, but it had not fulfilled her in the deepest sense of the word.

Fulfilment meant Scott. Her happiness was bound up with his.

For a full half-hour she soaked her aches and pains away, then towelled herself off and slipped into a peach satin nightdress and matching robe. She couldn't help thinking about the way Scott had kissed her. All the old sweetness and tenderness had returned. For long moments it seemed he had trusted her, his faith restored. Her lack of numbness surprised her, confirmation that her body was returning to full strength.

She was looking around for Abe's liniment when there was a knock on the door. Whatever Peter's reservations, Alex knew the liniment was highly beneficial. It soaked deep into the skin, leaving only a silky softness with no residual trace of oiliness.

Alex padded across the carpet, expecting to find Wyn, only it was Scott who looked down at her with a taut, complex expression.

"How's it going?" he asked. "No pain? No swelling in the leg?"

She shook her head, masses of curls bouncing from the humidity of the bath. "A few aches and pains. Nothing I can't handle. I told you I'm a veteran." She held the rolled collar of her robe, a delicate hand to her throat.

"May I come in?"

"Of course." She turned away. "How's Wyn? The day's experience took a lot out of her."

"I sent her off to bed. We have a big weekend coming up. By the way, the hospital rang. Peter's resting comfortably. It wasn't a bad break. I might get someone to pick him up tomorrow and bring him back for a few days before he goes home."

"That'll be nice." Alex picked up her hairbrush, drew it through her hair in an effort to subdue it.

"You look glowing," he said.

"A bubble bath." She gave him a soft smile.

"I would have thought that ride would have exhausted you," he said, picking up an ornament and putting it down again.

"Knowing *you* were safe gave me back all my energy." She went to a drawer, found the liniment. "I was just going to massage my leg."

"I'll do it for you."

"You want it healed?"

"Of course I do, Alex. What a thing to say."

"Even if I go away?"

"Shut up," he said quietly.

"I'll get a towel." Already she could feel his magical touch on her skin.

She took a fresh towel from the bathroom, brought it back into the lovely bedroom.

"Lie down," Scott said. "Are you going to get rid of that robe?"

"I'm only wearing my nightie."

"I know what you look like."

"I haven't forgotten. Are you sure you know what you're doing?" she teased.

"It can't be too difficult." He positioned the pink towel where her legs would rest. "This is Abe's liniment, isn't it?"

"It does a wonderful job. Magic, I swear."

He took the stopper off, sniffed it. "It smells marvellous, as well. What the heck is it?"

"Abe won't tell."

At his first touch she thought her body would melt.

"Hey, keep still," he jeered softly, aqua eyes gleaming. He splashed a little more liniment into his palm and rubbed his hands together. It released a fragrance not fruity, floral or herbal, but more of incense.

Alex pulled up the hem of her long nightgown so it exposed her legs to the thigh.

Gently, *lovingly*, surely? He began to massage the limb from knee to ankle.

"How does that feel?" He looked down at her, his expression undeniably sensual.

"*Extraordinary*."

"Your skin is like satin."

With his every sliding movement, the heat was rising

in her, spreading out and through her body like a flower bursting open.

"Do you think I should do the other leg?" he asked rather dryly.

"Why not?" She was too far gone to stop him until with a shuddering rush she tipped her head back, holding one hand to her forehead. "This is *so good*, it's sinful."

"Do you want me to stop?" The inflection in his voice tore at her senses.

"I think you'd better, don't you?"

"I suppose." His fingers teased the satin-bound hem of her nightgown where it rested back against her thigh.

"Why did you do such a crazy thing today? You could have put your whole life in jeopardy." His handsome face was intense, sculptured with light.

"I've told you a thousand times, Scott. *I love you.*"

All of a sudden he was kissing her, moving sideways onto the bed and pulling her into his arms, her body straining towards his.

"I missed you every minute, every second you were away," he muttered against her open mouth.

"But I'm home."

He shuddered, his splendid head upflung. "Take care what you say, Alex."

"I'm saying I don't ever want to go away again." She held his eyes, saw the deep uncertainty flash across his face.

"Have you forgotten your ambitions?" His voice was harsh with tension.

"Whatever they were, they've been fulfilled."

There was a certain hardness about him, the characteristic glitter. "Don't play games with me, Alex."

She sat up, put out her hand. "Darling, listen to me for a minute. I love you. I want to stay with you."

"My God, Alex," he said. "You drive me *crazy*!"

"Don't you hear me?" she begged, trying to convince him.

"Alex, I can't go through all the old misery again. Neither can I live like this. What is it you want of me?"

"I want us to start afresh," she cried emotionally, her heart in her eyes. "What happened between us happened. We've both learned something. Our lives are inextricably linked. There's nothing for either of us without the other."

"You're saying you'll marry me?" His beautiful eyes were brushed with exultation.

"There's nothing in the world I want more. All I am, all I'll ever be, is yours."

"And your dancing?" His tone held regret. "God, you're so good. It was wrong to deny you. I know that now. I should have—"

She stopped him, her fingers to his lips. "Don't, Scott. We've both come a long way."

"And your escape route is closed." He swept her into his arms, her vivid, forceful Scott. "We've come full circle, my love."

EPILOGUE

ON THE night of the gala dinner, Stephanie, supremely elegant in her two-piece suit cut from a sumptuous silver brocade, stood up, her startling aquamarine eyes shining with pride and delight.

"Dear family and friends," she began, ringing a little crystal bell to call for attention. Immediately a hush fell over everyone around the beautifully appointed table. They all looked towards her, waiting for her to speak. It was obvious Stephanie was revelling in the spotlight. She had something of a reputation as a witty after-dinner speaker and she was well-known for being able to turn any situation to her advantage. Now she smiled down the long, gleaming table at her splendid son, Scott, and at Alexandra, exquisite in gold lace, to his right. "I have a special announcement to make," she said. "I'm so excited I can't contain it any longer. It's with the greatest joy I announce the engagement of my beloved Scott to our dearest Alexandra, who is as you know Wyn's greatly gifted goddaughter."

Waves of applause, a few gasps, undisguised delight. No one had ever seen Scott look so totally happy, so vivid, so alive, or his beautiful Alexandra so radiant with joy. It was a light, an actual aura that clung to her, making her glow.

The engagement would be short, Stephanie went on to tell them. A little under six months, allowing sufficient time for such a big wedding to be arranged. It was apparent to all she was thrilled, very much the devoted mother on hand to direct the big event, when everyone at the table knew Stephanie had been gone for years and years, leaving Scott's Aunt Edwina to do the real mothering.

Someone in fact said so. "You should be doing that," the distinguished man seated beside Wyn murmured in an aside.

"She is his mother, Bruno." Wyn smiled serenely into her companion's fine dark eyes. She was still feeling stunned by the fact he was here. It was actually a miracle. Something she had dreamed about but accepted could never happen. Yet Bruno, Stephanie's mystery guest, was sitting beside her, looking as though he had recovered a prized possession. Bruno Adamski, known to the country at large as Brent Adamson, the millionaire property developer.

My lost love, Wyn thought. The man my father firmly believed was nothing more than a fortune-hunter. Well, her father had been wrong. That evening of evenings, Wyn threw off forever a long-abiding sadness. Bruno was still handsome; indeed he had considerable presence. He had made his own fortune many times over and was now a widower with grandchildren. Wyn had known from the first moment they had been reintroduced by a conspiratorial Stephanie with the sheen of real tears in her eyes, that Bruno hadn't forgotten her any more than she had succeeded in forgetting him.

"At least I must thank Stephanie for bringing us back together," Bruno said, renewing the bond that had been forged so long ago. Under cover of the general gaiety, the warm voices, the congratulations, he rested his hand over Wyn's, so warming her heart that rosy colour rushed to her cheeks. "Somewhere along the line, Stephanie put two and two together and came up with the right answer. She said it was my eyes that gave me away. The eyes and voice. I've never lost all trace of my accent. I didn't think she would remember me. Almost nobody does.''

"I'd have known you anywhere,'' Wyn said very gently, keeping for later how she had tracked his meteoric rise over the years. "Even now it's hard to realise it's been so long. My heart feels like it was only yesterday.''

"As does mine,'' he said in a voice that had a deep, tender quality to it. "Your family separated us, *cara*. Your family brought us back together. For that I am forever in Stephanie's debt.''

"Oh, Bruno, don't. I think I'll cry,'' Wyn warned him shakily.

"I don't see anything wrong with that,'' he said, smiling. "So long as you cry in my arms.''

Later, photographs were taken. One especially happy one showed Alex smiling into Scott's eyes as though the love light reflected there was the most brilliant light of all. The newly engaged couple was flanked by Stephanie arm in arm with a McLaren uncle and Wyn, who was reaching out to a handsome, dignified-looking man with a thick thatch of steel grey hair. The well-known entrepreneur, Brent Adamson. Though it came as a surprise to many, it was obvious the two of them were good friends though it wasn't absolutely clear from when. In fact, at that precise moment they looked a lot more than friends.

"No one deserves happiness more than Wyn!'' Alex said dreamily to Scott, her head resting against his heart. "Who would have thought your mother would produce Wyn's enduring love out of the blue. It's almost too much to grasp.''

"For that alone I can forgive her," Scott murmured, keeping his gaze on his aunt. "Look at Wyn now. She's walking on air."

"I know the feeling." Alex tipped up her face for his kiss. "There is a pattern. A meaning to life."

An enormous lightness seized him. A joy that had him soaring like an eagle in a cloudless blue sky. So much to give thanks for. "Alexandra, I love you," he said, blue-green eyes blazing.

And that was the way it remained for the sum of his days.

**MARGARET WAY is a romance legend—
one of the most popular romance writers
ever published! If you love her books,
don't miss *The Australian Heiress*!**

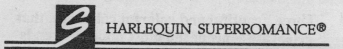

HARLEQUIN SUPERROMANCE®

**Superromance is proud to welcome
Margaret Way and to present her first *long* book:**

THE AUSTRALIAN HEIRESS

Camilla Guildford is the daughter—and heiress—
of a powerful Australian financier. But she hasn't inherited
the fortune everyone *thinks* she has. Instead, her father's
death has left her with an unexpected legacy of bitterness.

She blames one man for her father's decline.
Nick Lombard. Can you fall in love with your enemy?

Look for *The Australian Heiress* (#762)
from Superromance in November 1997.

Available wherever Harlequin books are sold.

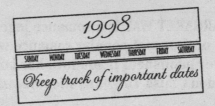

1998

SUNDAY MONDAY TUESDAY WEDNESDAY THURSDAY FRIDAY SATURDAY

Keep track of important dates

Three beautiful and colorful calendars that celebrate some of the most popular trends in America today.

Look for:

Just Babies—a 16 month calendar that features a full year of absolutely adorable babies!

1998 CALENDAR
Just Babies
16 months of adorable bundles of joy!

Hometown Quilts
1998 Calendar
A 16 month quilting extravaganza!

Hometown Quilts—a 16 month calendar featuring quilted art squares, plus a short history on twelve different quilt patterns.

Inspirations—a 16 month calendar with inspiring pictures and quotations.

Inspirations

A 16 month calendar that will lift your spirits and gladden your heart

Steeple Hill™

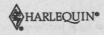

HARLEQUIN®

Value priced at $9.99 U.S./$11.99 CAN., these calendars make a perfect gift!

Available in retail outlets in August 1997.   CAL98

HARLEQUIN WOMEN KNOW ROMANCE WHEN THEY SEE IT.

And they'll see it on **ROMANCE CLASSICS**, the new 24-hour TV channel devoted to romantic movies and original programs like the special **Harlequin® Showcase of Authors & Stories.**

The **Harlequin® Showcase of Authors & Stories** introduces you to many of your favorite romance authors in a program developed exclusively for Harlequin® readers.

Watch for the **Harlequin® Showcase of Authors & Stories** series beginning in the summer of 1997.

If you're not receiving ROMANCE CLASSICS,
call your local cable operator or satellite provider
and ask for it today!

Escape to the network of your dreams.

ROMANCE CLASSICS

The Gentleman & The Hell Raiser

Don't miss these captivating stories
from two acclaimed authors
of historical romance.

THE GENTLEMAN by Kristin James
THE HELL RAISER by Dorothy Glenn

Two brothers on a collision course
with destiny and love.

Find out how the dust settles October 1997
wherever Harlequin and Silhouette
books are sold.

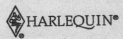 

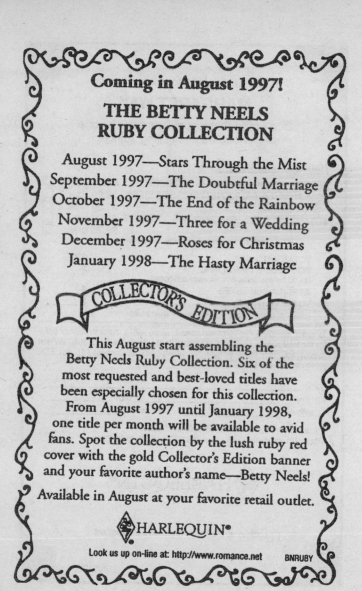

Coming in August 1997!

THE BETTY NEELS
RUBY COLLECTION

August 1997—Stars Through the Mist
September 1997—The Doubtful Marriage
October 1997—The End of the Rainbow
November 1997—Three for a Wedding
December 1997—Roses for Christmas
January 1998—The Hasty Marriage

COLLECTOR'S EDITION

This August start assembling the
Betty Neels Ruby Collection. Six of the
most requested and best-loved titles have
been especially chosen for this collection.
From August 1997 until January 1998,
one title per month will be available to avid
fans. Spot the collection by the lush ruby red
cover with the gold Collector's Edition banner
and your favorite author's name—Betty Neels!

Available in August at your favorite retail outlet.

HARLEQUIN®

If you are looking for more titles by

MARGARET WAY

Don't miss these popular stories by one
of Harlequin's bestselling authors:

Harlequin Romance®

#03295	ONE FATEFUL SUMMER	$2.99 U.S.	☐
#03391	A FAULKNER POSSESSION	$2.99 U.S.	☐
		$3.50 CAN.	☐
#03455	GEORGIA AND THE TYCOON	$3.25 U.S.	☐
		$3.75 CAN.	☐

(limited quantities available on certain titles)

TOTAL AMOUNT	$
POSTAGE & HANDLING	$
($1.00 for one book, 50¢ for each additional)	
APPLICABLE TAXES*	$ _____
TOTAL PAYABLE	$ _____

(check or money order—please do not send cash)

To order, complete this form and send it, along with a check or money order
for the total above, payable to Harlequin Books, to: **In the U.S.:** 3010 Walden
Avenue, P.O. Box 9047, Buffalo, NY 14269-9047; **In Canada:** P.O. Box 613,
Fort Erie, Ontario, L2A 5X3.

Name: _____

Address: _____ City: _____

State/Prov.: _____ Zip/Postal Code: _____

*New York residents remit applicable sales taxes.
Canadian residents remit applicable GST and provincial taxes.

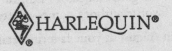

HARLEQUIN®

Look us up on-line at: http://www.romance.net

HMWBACK4